Love Finds a Way

First printing: 2019

ISBN: 978-1-7339577-1-7

MRosales Novels
https://www.facebook.com/MRosalesNovels/

Chapter 1

It was cold and dark and all I wanted was to be asleep in my bed. The party inside was blaring, but for the life of me I could never fit in with that crowd, not anymore that is. My ride left half an hour ago without any sense of telling me, plus I had no money for a bus ride, so I walked home. I listened to the calm pitter patter of the rain as it began to fall on the silent world around me. I cherished the time alone. Ever since the accident I've been bombarded with unnecessary socialization. I finally crawl into bed around three in the morning, and it wasn't until a knock at my door that I woke up.

"What is it?" "Breakfast" sang a soft voice from the other side of the door. Great it was my older sister Haley. "Come in," I mumble. She carried in a tray that revealed a bowl of cereal and a cup of orange juice and carefully placed it on my nightstand. "So where did you go last night?" "Don't worry about it Haley." "Well I was thinking maybe we could go to the mall or something, maybe get our nails done. What do you think?" Haley said excitedly. "I don't think so Haley, I don't feel like it." She pauses for a moment, giving me a look of disappointment, and then continuing. "Look Sarah, you've been slugging around like your life is so terrible. It's been seven months since the accident and it's time you move on with your life already. You keep waiting for something that will never happen. He's gone, why can't you comprehend that?" I was on the verge of crying, but my tears turn to anger. "Sarah I'm sor…" "Get out now!" I did not want to hear this right now. I point to the door and without another word she leaves.

Once she leaves, I get up and change into some fresh clothes. As I stare into the mirror, I could tell the tan I worked so hard to get was now starting to fade. My sandy blonde hair is a horrid mess of tangles, and my blue eyes have dark bags under them from lack of sleep. When I finish getting ready, I lock my door and sneak out the window.

I didn't want to, but it has been four weeks since I have gone to see him. I make my way to the cemetery, unsure if I'll be able to control myself, but who cares. Nothing really matters anymore. Once I enter through the gates, I make my way to his grave, feeling the sorrow grow stronger with each step. Then right there in front of me stood his tombstone, with big letters reading "In loving memory of Jake Henson." I began to wonder, why was it so unfair? He is gone, and I am still here. I know why, I was being taught a lesson, a lesson that would make me suffer each day, and I deserved every second of it. I couldn't hold it in anymore. I drop to my knees and start to cry. Jake was my first relationship and the only guy I could say I loved. He was my first everything, and when I found out he was gone, it was like my heart had been ripped out of my chest. The feeling of losing someone you love, someone who means the world to you, is probably the worst feeling anyone could ever feel. I would not wish it upon my worst enemy. The longer I sat there, the more looks I got from people passing by, so I pull myself together and make my way home.

As I approach the porch steps, I can see my mom through the window, pacing back and forth with a frantic look on her face. "Where the hell have you been?" She screams as I enter the house. "The cemetery, do you have a problem with that?" "As a matter of fact I do! You can't just run off without telling anyone, you had me worried sick." "Well lucky for you mom, I'm still here!" I head for the stairs, retreating to my room. "It wouldn't hurt you to be nice every once in a while, we are just looking out for you" she shouts. I slam my door and fall onto my bed, screaming into my pillow, trying to release my frustration, and in turn fall asleep.

I wake up around six and head downstairs. I figure I can apologize by helping my mom make dinner. When I get to the edge of the stairs, I see Dr. Loucheski sitting at our kitchen table. Dr. Loucheski is my therapist. He's tall, slender, middle aged, has a mustache that makes him look like a pedophile, and for being a grown man he sure has a mousey voice.

I make my presence known by clearing my throat. I can tell I startled them by the expressions on their face. "What are you all talking about?" I ask. "We were just discussing some things" my father replies. "Like what? If it's about me don't you think I should be here too?" "Sarah please settle down, we just need to figure out what's best for you right now, this whole incident has really changed you." My mother tells me. "Oh well I'm sorry mom, you're not the one who has to live with the fact they're a murderer."

"Sarah" interrupted Dr. Loucheski. "Have you been taking your medications?" Damn I haven't taken those for a month. "No" I said firmly, "I can't sleep when I do." "Well I could prescribe you some that…" "No! I just want everyone to leave me alone!" I shout. They were speechless. "Please have a seat Sarah." Dr. Loucheski says as he motions toward the chair. I could tell they were hiding something, and I wasn't going to like it. "Just tell me what's going on" I demand. "Your parents and I" says Dr. Loucheski, while giving a cautious look to my parents, then continues, "think you should move to Los Angeles with your grandparents. Just to try see if a new environment helps you cope better." "What?" I say dumbfounded. I couldn't believe it, the two people who are supposed to care for me and love me no matter what, are trying to get rid of me. "Am I that much of a problem?" "Not at all sweetie, you just need to get away from here for a while to take time to refresh and separate yourself from all of the havoc surrounding you here. "Your father's right" my mother agrees, "this place is full of bad memories and it's just holding you back from so many things." "But…" "It's too late Sarah, the plans have been arranged, and you will leave in two weeks." Dr. Loucheski states. At that moment I wanted to reach across the table and rip that stupid mustache off his face. I didn't know what else to say, so I stood up and went to take a shower.

I stand there, motionless, letting the hot water roll down my body. The warmth feels good, it makes me feel safe. I wish all my tears and pains could just go down the drain with the water. It's not like I enjoy feeling this way. It's not my fault that none of the therapies or medications have eased my depression, like they promised countless times.

The next two weeks consist of packing and saying my good-byes. I tried to convince myself this was going to be a fresh start for me. I'll get to meet a bunch of new people, get a chance to know my dad's parents, and maybe pick up where I left off in college. Who am I kidding? Ever since the accident I've pretty much shut everyone out of my life and have become a hermit. In my perspective Los Angeles is just a big city, constantly buzzing with life, there's no way I'll fit in there.

Chapter 2

Great my last night here and I have the nightmare. I have the nightmare at least, four times a week and it's always the same thing, it never changes.

It's pitch black. I'm standing alone in the middle of the street.

There's a single lamppost, the light is barely flickering.

In the distance a figure of a man appears.

I walk towards him. As I get closer, I see that it's Jake. My walk turns into a sprint. "Jake" I scream, he turns in my direction and smiles at me.

When I reach out to touch him, he vanishes. I'm alone again.

My tears turn into rain drops, and my screams match the beats of thunder.

I wake up covered in sweat, get a drink of water, and lay back down.

The next morning my dad and Haley offer to drop me off at the airport. My mom however, thought it would be too hard for her to say good-bye so she watched from the window as we drove off. No kiss, no tears, just a wave. I bet she is relieved to get rid of me. Haley is taking it the hardest. She won't let me go and keeps pleading with dad to let me stay. We both know it isn't up to him. Dr. Loucheski is the one in charge, so whatever he says goes. Seeing her cry made me want to cry. We use to be super close, before the accident. We had done almost everything together and she was the first one I would go to for anything. We were more than sisters, we were best friends. It makes me regret being such a jerk to her, especially knowing that after today, who knows when I'll see her next. My dad simply hugs me, kisses me on my forehead, and tells me he loves me no matter what. Then they both wish me a safe trip, indicating that it is time for me to go. Next thing I know, I am boarding the plane and heading to Los Angeles.

Chapter 3

The first time I saw Jake was the eighth grade when he walked into my Math class labeled as the 'new kid.' Of course, no one had a chance to make fun of him. He gained instant popularity with the guys for being on the football team and his good looks and personality made him popular amongst the girls.

I didn't get to actually meet him until the ninth grade when we had English together. Our teacher partnered us up to write a report over Romeo & Juliet. Coincidence? I think not. Ironic? Maybe a little, but it didn't take long for me to fall for him. His smile and the way he talked about life swept me off my feet. Luckily after the report was over, we still managed to hang out. He would come over every day after football so we could do homework together. Mom and Dad loved him. That summer we started dating, and by time school started up again we were in love.

Jake was one of a kind. His tan body and wavy dark brown hair with blue eyes made him look like a Greek God. He was so optimistic about everything and he could make a person he just met laugh so hard it would make them cry. He was smart, athletic, and kind hearted. He was friends with anyone and everyone, he didn't have a single enemy.

Spontaneous was also a good word to describe Jake. He would always leave a note in my locker on Friday's telling me when and where to meet him and what we were going to do each weekend. We did this every weekend and each week it would be something different. It made me look forward to the weekend even more than I already did.

However, with every good there is of course a bad. Ms. Henson, Jake's mother, wasn't very fond of me. Actually, hate is a pretty strong word and that's exactly how she felt about me. She wanted Jake to have a more sophisticated, natural looking girlfriend with good-morals. Instead he brought home me, this Barbie doll looking, loud mouth that barely made the honor roll. She always found a way to blame me for when Jake's grades were slipping or for him not getting enough sleep. This is probably why after Jake's death she got a restraining order for me to stay away from her and her house. This didn't affect me since half his stuff was at my house anyway.

After graduation, Jake accepted a scholarship to the University of Kentucky for football. Fortunately, the community college I enrolled in was in Lexington as well, making it to where we could both live at home during school. I knew Jake wasn't happy with his decision. In his heart he wanted to pursue marine biology, but his mom told him it was a worthless degree that would get him nowhere in life and strongly encouraged him to get a business degree. Even though it meant Jake would have to move away, I told him he needed to follow his heart, but all he said was 'My heart is wherever you are Sarah.' He always put others first, and that's why I promised myself, one day I would take him to the ocean just so he could see what he was missing.

Our relationship had its trials and tribulations but our love for one another never faltered. Jake was my everything. We had our whole future planned ahead of us. But I guess fate had different plans.

Chapter 4

When I make it to the baggage claim I can see Hector, my grandparent's butler. I should have known Hector was picking me up since my grandparents don't have time for things like picking up their granddaughter at the airport. Which is completely alright, now that I'm used to it after 22 years.

The odd thing is me and Hector have always gotten along well. As I approach him though, he looks saddened. He's probably overheard all the commotion about me. "Hello Miss Sarah." "Hey Hector." I say giving him a half smile. "How about we get you to your grandparent's house eh?" he says as he takes my bags from me. "Good idea." I mumble.

We don't speak another word until we arrive at my grandparents. "Here we are" he says, as we pull up to the iron gates guarding the entrance to the house. I always forget how charming their house is. On the outside the house looks almost Victorian with vines growing along the side, and the elegant water fountain gives it a more modern look. Once you enter the house it looks more like a show home, as if no one actually lives here. I wonder how long it will take for me to adapt.

"Sarah darling, it's so nice to see you" exclaims my grandma as she kisses each side of my cheek "how are you?" Sometimes I wonder about my grandma, I mean how does she think I'm doing? Does she remember the reason why I'm here? "I'm fine, how are you?" "I'm good, work's been keeping me busy though, I got a deadline coming up you know?" "Oh?" I say, "that must be stressful." "It certainly can be at times" she says as she makes her way to the end of the staircase. My grandma helps write movie scripts for some big time directors in Hollywood, which is mainly how my grandparents get all their money, but my grandpa also makes a lot of money from selling his artwork. It's pretty crazy but it's what they live for.

"Ralph" my grandma screams, "Sarah's here!" I see my grandpa emerge from the library. When he is not in his studio you can usually find him in there 'broadening the aspects of his mind' as he calls it.

"Why, hello sweet pea" he says as he kisses my forehead, "how was your flight?" "It was good, but if you don't mind I'm gonna go get settled in?" I reply. "Of course not, make yourself at home." "Esther will have dinner ready at 6:30" grandma adds. "Thanks." I say as I proceed to the guest room, which I guess is technically now my room.

I set my bags down on my huge king sized bed and start to put my clothes away. As I'm hanging up my pants I notice a piece of paper in one of the pants pockets. It's a poem Jake had written me.

Sarah oh Sarah, where is my dear Sarah

I need my Sarah so I can tell her how amazing she is

And how her smile makes me smile

And how every time I look into her eyes I fall in love all over again

So if you see my Sarah dear please tell her I love her dear

Love, Jake

I thought it was so corny when he first gave it to me, but honestly I would kill for another one of those. I fold it back up and put it in my nightstand. I finish unpacking and then head downstairs for dinner.

I couldn't wait for dinner because from what I remember Esther is one of the best cooks in all of Los Angeles, in my opinion of course. Esther is my grandparent's chef and anything she cooks is absolutely delicious. Tonight we are having stuffed ravioli with cheese drizzled over the top and for dessert, a chocolate bunt cake.

After dinner we all go our separate ways, respecting that none of us wish to be bothered. I turn on the TV and flip through the channels, but nothing worth watching is on. I turn the TV off and head upstairs. I lay on my bed, staring at the ceiling and thinking about everything that's happened. I recall the day I lost Jake forever, the month I spent in the hospital, and the months following the accident, and everything I've gone through since the night of the accident. It all seemed so unreal, as if it was all just a bad dream and eventually I'd wake up. That is not the case though, it was pure reality. That's when it really hits people. When you finally grasp that it just isn't some dream, it's real whether you like it or not and you can't change anything about it, but hey, that's life.

All that thinking must have put me to sleep because next thing I know, my clock reads 9:36 a.m. and I hear a bunch of commotion from downstairs. I slowly get out of bed, contemplating if I should take a shower or not. I decide to take a shower, so I gather my clothes and head for the bathroom. I try to be quick, but also making sure I wash my neck good since the cheap chain to my necklace stains my neck a slight green. In all honesty though, this necklace could turn my whole neck green but I'd never take it off. This necklace holds something valuable.

When I get downstairs grandpa's reading the newspaper and drinking coffee. "Good morning Sarah, help yourself to some orange juice and breakfast if you'd like." "Thanks grandpa." I say, as I make my way to the counter. "Where's grandma?" I ask. "She went to go present one of her scripts to some company's downtown. Did you need to talk to her?" "Oh no, I was just curious." He looks at his watch, then looks up at me. "Well I hate to run out on you too, but there's an exhibit that needs criticizing. You're welcome to come with me if you'd like."

"That's okay grandpa, I think I might pass so I can relax some." "Of course sweet pea, but it is a magnificent day outside. Feel free to go down to the beach if you want and I'll leave some money with Hector in case you decide to go shopping." "That's very generous of you, but I couldn't take your money grandpa." He walks over to me and kisses me on the forehead, "what's mine is yours Sarah. Your grandma and I are so happy to have you here" he tells me and leaves without another word.

I didn't want to take the offer but after two hours that consisted of browsing the internet, painting my nails, and writing in my journal, I was running out of options. I go to my room and change into my bikini. I stop and stare at myself in the mirror, taking notice of each scar. I use my index finger to trace over the one that runs from my hip down to my thigh. I shutter and wonder how anyone could ever find someone as battered and bruised as me, attractive. I look like a monster. I am a monster. Dr. Loucheski says my scars are a symbol of strength and represent overcoming challenges. To me they represent weakness and painful memories. I quickly put on some clothes and make my way to the basement, or in other words, Hector's room.

I knock on the door and wait for a response. After a minute of silence I crack open the door, "Hello. Hector, are you down here?" He quickly emerges from around the corner, "Hello Sarah, what can I do for you?" "Well if you aren't too busy I was wondering if you could take me to the beach?" "Let's go" he tells me as he grabs the keys off the hook.

As we pull up I become awestruck. I forgot how beautiful it was here. "Welp, this is your stop," Hector says, snapping me back to reality. "I'll be back to get you around five, is that enough time?" "That's plenty" I say as I get out of the car. I turn to watch him drive off and instantly regret not asking him to stay with me. Now I'm stuck in the middle of this buying crowd, not knowing a single person or where to go.

I make my way down the board walk and soon become intrigued by some of the stores. One has a bunch of cool shell necklaces and bracelets and another has a bunch of tourist trinkets that are way over priced. The last store I happen across is a scuba diving shop and as I'm browsing through the different equipment I hear a frantic "look out" come from behind me. It's too late though, I am knocked down by some guy on a skateboard.

"Oh my gosh, I am so sorry!" The guy exclaims as he helps me up. "I wasn't expecting anyone to be in here, we are supposed to be closed." "Oh" I say, "I didn't know, the door was unlocked." "Dammit, I've told Rick a million times to lock the door when he leaves" he whispers to himself. "I'm sorry, I'll just leave." I tell him. "No! I mean, uh, it's cool. It's not like we get much business in here anyway" he says trying to convince me to stay. "Which makes me wonder, are you new around here?" "Uhm sort of" I reply. Great I didn't want to get in this conversation right now. "Oh, well right on" he says while giving me a charming grin. This is the first time I take account of his appearance. He is a few inches taller than me with blonde shaggy hair and blue eyes. His smile though, there is something about it that I just couldn't shake but I can't figure out what it is. I was waiting for the dreaded question of *why are you here,* but to my surprise he didn't press the subject. Instead, he picks up his skateboard and walks to the back room. I stand there trying to process what happened but I can't come up with a rational answer so I shake my head and leave before he comes back out. At this point, I still have two hours to kill so I make my way down by the beach.

When I make it down by the ocean, there is a group of people playing volleyball and a few surfers getting ready to go into the water. I sit
down not far from the shore line, just close enough to let the water
splash up to my feet and watch the surfers. I am mesmerized by their
skill and ability to do such a fascinating activity. It isn't long until the
alarm on my phone goes off so I make my way back up to the where
Hector dropped me off. When I make it up there, he is already there
waiting for me. As we were walking to the limo I remember the promise
I made to Jake. He had always wanted to go to the beach. He swore that
he was meant to be by the ocean, which is why he wanted to be a marine
biologist. He would have loved it here.

"Did you enjoy your time today?" Hector asks me. "For the most
part" I reply. He stops walking and puts his hand on my shoulder while
looking me in the eyes. "I'm not saying things will get better right away,
but eventually they will. That doesn't mean the pain or the love will go
away either. But with time, you will heal and eventually you will be able
to move on." "But how do I know when I'm ready to move on?" I croak.
"Because there will become a point when you ask yourself, would I ex-

pect him to stay miserable the rest of his life? The answer is no Sarah. He may not be the one that gets to make you happy, but that doesn't mean he doesn't want you to be happy. He knows at one point you loved him and you probably always will, and that's enough to appease him as he watches over you now." He has a good point, but it hurt too much to hear. The whole way home, his words kept replaying in my head, but I knew it wasn't that simple. No one understood, they never would. Even if I tried to explain it to people they would still try to convince me that we were high school sweethearts that liked the thought of being in love rather than actually being in love. Which is the furthest away from being true. What we had was special. The love we shared was one of a kind, the kind that only comes along when even God knows two people are meant for each other. That is until he changes his mind and separates them forever.

As I walk through the doors of the house I can already smell Esther making dinner. I continue into the living room and see my grandpa sitting on the couch watching a football game. I try to sneak past, but to my surprise he is very vigilant. "Why hello Sarah, care to join me?" Not wanting to seem rude I make my way to the couch and sit next to him. "Hi grandpa" I say. "Well I certainly know where you went today." "Huh?" I reply. "I can tell you went to the beach. You got yourself a bit of sun." "Oh, I didn't even notice." I tell him as I look down at my own arms and legs. "Did you enjoy yourself?" He asks. "Yeah, it was pretty fun" I reply, "oh and here's your money back, I didn't use any of it." I go to hand him the money but he doesn't move. "Keep it, you can use it to buy some new school clothes." I put the money back in my pocket. "Thank you grandpa. If you don't mind, I was going to take a quick shower before dinner" I say as I stand to make my escape. "Would it be too much to ask for a hug?" he asks. Now I really felt bad, I give him a hug, "thanks for everything grandpa."

I make my way to the bathroom for a quick shower since I had sand in areas I'd rather not mention. When I come out of the bathroom I bump into my grandma. "Oh goodness I'm sorry sweetie, I must really start paying attention to where I'm going" she exclaims. "It's alright, it wouldn't be the first time today" I reply. "What do you mean?" She asks. I explain to her the scenario between me and the guy on the skateboard earlier. "Oh my, did he apologize?" I couldn't help but laugh at how sincere her reaction was. "Yes grandma, he even helped me up too." "Well hmph, he should be more careful with that board thing of his." Before we can say anything else we are interrupted by the dinner bell. After dinner I go to my room and pass out from exhaustion. Today was probably the most active I had been in months and it wore me out.

When I wake up I don't feel like getting out of bed, but I have no choice since there is a lot to do today. First on the list is to enroll at my new school. How am I supposed to transfer to a new school with only a semester left of my degree? Not to mention, having no familiar faces around. At least everyone in Kentucky already knows my story and I don't have to try and pretend to be someone I'm not. Moving to California was the worst idea ever.

Wow this school is huge, I think to myself as Hector drops me off. I am going to get so lost on my first day. After getting directions from multiple people, I finally find myself in the enrollment office.

"Hi, can I help you?" The receptionist asks. "Um, yes, I need to enroll for the fall semester." "Alrighty then, are you a returning Spartan or a new member to our pack." "Uhm..." She lets out a chuckle, "I can tell by the look on your face you're new to the school. Let me grab the right paperwork for you, and if you don't mind having a seat over there I'll be back in just a minute." As I wait I look around the room, taking account of all the championship trophies, awards, and certificates. I can tell from what I see that the school is athletically driven. I wonder how good their soccer program is, even though I know I'd probably never play again. "Alright, this should be all you need, if you could fill it out for me then I can get it processed today. If you have any questions my name is Tabitha." "Okay thanks" I say and make my way back to my seat and begin to fill out all the papers. When I am done she helps me set up my schedule. Which I'm not going to lie, I am kind of excited for. This school definitely offers way more opportunities than my old school. Looks like I will be taking Business Communications, Microcomputer Applications, Principles of Advertising, and Introduction to Investments and that will get me my Associates of Business Administration.

It is 2p.m. by time I leave the school and next on the list is job hunting. My grandparents proposed to buy me a car as long as I got a job to pay for the gas and insurance. At first, I refused but they said I would not be able to use Hector for my everyday use and that if they didn't spend their money on this then what else would they spend it on. As much as I wanted the latest Mustang I felt the responsible thing to do is get a nice, reasonable car. So I finally agreed to letting them get me an adorable SUV. I think my grandparents were quite surprised I didn't go for the finer selection of cars but I think they were pretty humbled by my choice. It feels weird though, being this spoiled, especially when I am so undeserving of it all.

After five places turning me down due to full employment I begin to feel hopeless and end up just walking along the boardwalk. I watch as everyone moves about, enjoying themselves, like there isn't a worry in the world. I remember being that carefree, now look where I am. I feel the urge to be alone so I am making my way to docks when I hear someone shout "hey new girl." I try to refrain from turning around but I cave in. When I turn around I see the guy from the shop yesterday jogging up to me.

"Hey" was all he manages to say while trying to catch his breath. "Uh hi" I reply. "Where ya headed?" he asks. "To the docks" I tell him. "Would you like some company?" I wasn't sure if he felt bad and was trying to be friendly or if it was him that needed the company, either way I didn't want to be rude so I agree. "I don't think I ever got your name" he tells me. "It's Sarah." "Well hello Sarah, I'm Jason, Jason Steele!" he says as he sticks his hand out for me to shake. "Did you just move here or are you just here for the summer?" "Unfortunately I just moved here" I tell him. "What brought you all the way here?" Shit, I regret letting him come along now. "It's complicated" is all I say. "Ah, gotcha. Well are you gonna be going to school while you're here?" "Yeah, I just enrolled at Pacific University this morning." "That's awesome! This will be my second semester there, but I'd be happy to show you around. What's your major?" "Business Administration." "No way! I am going for Business Management, I'm sure we will have some classes together!" "Yeah maybe." He pauses for a moment, "I get the feeling you don't talk much" he tells me. "Look, I said you could come along, I didn't say we could play 20 questions." He stops walking, "sorry for bothering you" he tells me and then turns to walk the opposite way. I watch him walk off, but then the guilt starts to overwhelm me. "Wait!" I shout. I felt bad, just because my life sucks doesn't mean I should take it out on a guy who was just trying to be friendly. "I'm sorry" I tell him as he approaches me once again, "this move hasn't been easy on me and I didn't mean to take it out on you." He gives me a half smile, "it's okay, I know how difficult things can be" he tells me. If only he knew.

"Follow me," Jason says as he leads me under the docks. He says that hardly anybody comes down here so it's like a private place for him to come and think about what's on his mind. We start talking about school again and discover that we do have Business Communications together. At least he was right about one thing. It is refreshing to know that I'll know at least one person at school. We both become quiet and when I look over at him I catch him staring at me. "I know it seems like a sore subject to talk about, but why did you move here?" He asks me. I pause for a long moment as I look into his eyes and something told me I could trust him. I let out a large sigh, "Eight months ago, I got into a bad accident and some legal trouble. My parents basically couldn't handle me at my worst, so with the help of my therapist, they decided to send me here to live with my grandparents." I look at him, waiting for the judgement to spread across his face, like I have seen it do with many people before. Not this time though, not with him. "I'm so sorry Sarah. Your parents are wrong for agreeing to send you away. This is when they need to be parents most of all." He then pulls me into a hug and I did what any normal person would do, I hugged him back. There was one thing for certain, Jason Steele isn't such a bad guy after all. I thank him and tell him I am ready to head back up since I was getting hungry. He suggests we go to this burger shack across the street.

As we make our way there, we come across a couple of guys playing soccer. "Can we watch for just a minute?" I ask him. "That's the guy's soccer team for our school" he says while rolling his eyes. "So" I say, "believe it or not but, I use to play soccer." "I don't doubt it, it's just that those guys can be some cocky jerks" he says. As I focus on the group of guys playing, a guy at the opposite end of the field catches my attention and I become frozen. I know exactly why he caught my eye. It's Jake, and that is my last thought before I become unconscious.

As I am coming to, I can hear Jason and an unknown voice bickering. "I yelled watch out dude, it's not my fault she's deaf." "Obviously
not loud enough because she's not deaf" Jason snaps back. "You
shouldn't have been over here anyway" another voice hastily adds.
"Hey, look she's waking up" another voice says.

When I open my eyes, the guy across the field was there beside
me. "Jake" I say as I reach out and touch his cheek. "Jake? Whose
Jake?" the guy asks looking around. "She's probably just confused right
now" Jason says. "Get her some water" the Jake look alike commands
one of his teammates. "What if she has amnesia?" Says another guy.
"Shut up" Jason says as he pushes his way through the circle of guys and
kneels next to me. "How are you feeling?" Jason asks me. "Well my
head hurts" the group of guys laugh. The guy I believe to be Jake then
helps me up. "I'm sorry, it looks like Randy needs a bit more practice"
he says giving who I assume is Randy a glare. I am speechless and I
can't quit staring. It was as if Jake was standing right there in front of me
but I know better. I watched him flat line on the bed right next to mine at
the hospital.

"H...hi" I manage to say. "Hi" he replies, "here's you some water."

"Thanks" I say as I take a sip. "You need to be more careful. A pretty

girl like you needs to be more aware of your surroundings." I can't help

it, but I give him a smile and it was the first time I have in eight months.

"Well it may not seem like it, but I use to play soccer, so I was

intrigued." "Use to?" "Well, I just moved here" I tell him. "So, I take it

you're gonna be new to Pacific U then?" I nod, "I just enrolled this

morning." "Well you should consider trying out for the ladies team, they

can use some better players" he tells me. "I'll keep that in mind" I say.

"Our school is untraditional though. Try outs are held the first week of

school and the season is year around instead of just in the spring."

Sheesh, that is a bit intense, but as I already noticed, the school is very

athletically endorsed. "Good to know" I tell him.

"Well I think we should let them get back to practice" Jason

chimes in, "besides we should really get you something to eat now."

"Good idea" I say. "See ya around" the guy tells me before he jogs off. I

follow Jason as we continue our journey to the burger shack. I couldn't

refrain from asking any longer. "So, who was that?" "Who?" "The guy who helped me up." "Oh. That's Thomas Carter. Captain of the guy's soccer team, ladies man, grade A douchebag." "Ah" I reply, but the only thing on my mind is the name Thomas Carter. It was surreal how much he looked like Jake. If I didn't know better, I would think life was just one giant game and when Jake died he re-spawned all the way here in Los Angeles. I knew this wasn't the case though, but for some reason my mind was trying to trick me into believing that Thomas is my Jake Henson and he just needed to be reminded.

"Earth to Sarah!" "Huh, what?" "the waitress asked you what you wanted to eat" Jason says. "Oh, uh just the cheesy deluxe burger with fries is fine" I tell the waitress. As she walks off Jason turns to me and gives me a serious look. "What?" I ask. "Are you alright? Ever since you were knocked out you've been acting weird." "I'm fine" I plead. "Okay, now tell me what's really wrong. Is your head still hurting you?" "No that's not it Jason." "Aha! So there is something bothering you. What is it?" "You are just going to think I'm crazy." "Oh who isn't a little crazy" he says then flashes me that dazzling smile again. "Alright, well…that Thomas guy looks just like this guy that I uh…used to date. Oh and he played football, I mean technically soccer is futbol, right?" I was starting to ramble. Jason gives me a concerned look, but if he only knew what I was really thinking he would probably think I belonged in the looney bin Dr. Loucheski has worked so hard to keep me out of. "So…you still have feelings for your ex and you think Thomas can fill that void? "

"No! I mean, sort of. Never mind, you wouldn't understand" I say defensively. I was trying to think of a way to explain this but even I knew I sounded crazy. I feel embarrassed and stupid, why would I tell a guy I barely know something so personal. "He died" I finally blurt out. "Oh Sarah, I don't know what to say, other than don't let your-self be fooled okay? Thomas may look like your ex but that doesn't mean it's him. Life doesn't work that way." "Yeah I know" I say, but I wasn't listening though. My mind became preoccupied with ways to get closer to Thomas, or in my mind, Jake. "This was really nice but I need to get going. I told my grandparents I wouldn't be out long" I say after taking the last bite of my burger. I lied, but I have some new errands that I needed to tend to. "Well I hope I didn't say anything to make you hate me already." "What? No, I just need to get going" I tell him. "Okay, well maybe we can hang-out tomorrow if you're not busy?" "Sure." I give him my number and then call Hector to pick me up.

On the way back home, I have Hector stop at a sporting good store so I can get some soccer gear, since all mine is back in Kentucky. I plan on trying out for the soccer team, that is a sure way of getting closer to Thomas. As I am walking to the car, the frozen yogurt shop I interviewed at called stating they want to hire me. There's another check mark off the to-do list. When we pull up to the house, there is a new SUV parked in the round about with a bow sitting on the hood. I see my grandparents didn't waste time fulfilling their promise. At least, I have a job so I won't have to keep taking their money for much longer.

As I walk into the house with all my bags my grandmother stares in confusion. "What is all this?" she asks. "Some soccer gear, I am going to try out for the college's soccer team." "Well how wonderful" Grandma exclaims. "And," I add "Frozen Swirls, called saying I could start work tomorrow. Now I can start paying you and grandpa back." "No, no, no! You don't worry about paying us back. Just use the money you make for yourself. Oh I can't wait to tell your grandpa he's going to be so happy for you." "Thanks grandma." "Did you happen to see your present in the driveway?" Grandma says giddily. "How could I miss it, "thank you so much grandma" I say, giving her a hug and a kiss on the cheek. "I think I'm going to change start practicing a little" I tell her. "By all means, practice away my soccer star" she says stepping aside to let me pass. I cringe at her words. I wouldn't say I'm that good.

I practice for about an hour and man I needed it. My dribbling is rusty and I don't think I've even worked out since the accident so my lungs could barely stand the cardio. When I enter the house, I notice my grandpa has been watching from the window. "My, my someone worked up a good sweat" grandpa says. "It's long overdue, but I plan on trying out for the universities soccer team so I need to get back in shape." I tell him. "That's wonderful news, I think that's a great idea."

"She also has more news," grandma adds as she appears out of the blue. "Oh yeah, the frozen yogurt shop I interviewed at called and said I could start tomorrow." "You're just on a roll aren't ya?" He says as he motions for a high five. "Also, I wanted to thank you for the car. I appreciate your generosity" I tell him.

Later that night I decide to do some low grade stalking as I get on my laptop and browse through Thomas' social media sites. I look at his pictures for over an hour, thinking to myself, could it be possible? There is an uncanny resemblance between the two but I think Thomas' personality would be the differentiating factor. That is why I needed to get to know him, so I can at least get the twisted closure that I felt I needed. I finally tell myself I need to get some rest since tomorrow will be my first day of work.

I wake up a little late, so there's no time for breakfast. Which was probably a good thing since I am so nervous that I will probably just throw it up anyway. When I arrive, my manager greets me and gives me a quick orientation before explaining the process of what I am supposed to do. After that she introduces me to my only other coworker, Stacy, and tells us I need to shadow Stacy for a couple days before I can work on my own.

"It's not so hard once you get the hang of it" she tells me, "we just have to make sure the store is clean and ring people's order up. If one of the machines break we just call this guy and he comes and fixes it." She hands me a business card. Stacy is a curvy brunette that is one or two inches shorter than me and seems to be really nice. "Tonight I'll show you how to close the store so that way you'll be comfortable doing it on your own. Any questions so far?" "Uh, not right now" I tell her. We have a bunch of customers come in around lunch time and I am so slow at ringing people up, but with each customer I get a better hang of it. On our lunch break we just put a 'be back soon' sign on the door and part our ways. As I sit at one of the tables and eat a corndog it dawns on me that I told Jason I would hang out today. I call him to apologize and explain the situation. Of course he is understanding and we plan to hang out once I get off. When we get back from lunch, things are slow, so Stacy and I have a chance to talk about things other than work. I find out she just graduated high school and this will be her first year at Pacific University. Her parents are divorced but she lives with her mom because they get along better. When she asks what brought me to California, I simply tell her I moved here for a fresh start. I ask if she is going to play any sports but she says she would like to be a team manager for one instead. I tell her my plan to try out for the soccer team and suggest she should try to be a manager for the girls' soccer team. She seems excited and willing. Maybe this means I'll have two friends at school. When it comes time to close, she shows me how to clean the floor, put the stools up, turn the machines off, and put the money and receipts in the safe so the manager can collect it in the morning. She proposes I shadow her one more day before I go on my own. I agree and we part our ways after exchanging numbers.

I told Jason I would wait for him on the strip, but as I am waiting for him to arrive, I spot Thomas outside one of the shops. I decide to make my way over and use this as an opportunity for some one on one interaction with him. As I approach him he looks up and gives me a smile. "Hey, how's your head?" He asks. "A lot better, thanks for your help by the way." "No problem, it's the least I could do" he tells me. "Oh and just so you know…" but before I can say anything else a girl walks up and loops her arm around his.

"Babe, I'm ready to go" she says in a whiny tone. "Alright, just a second Jess" he looks back at me, "what were you were you saying?" I feel embarrassed and crushed. "I, uh, just wanted to let you know I plan on trying out for the team." "That's awesome! The girls need all the help they can get, I'm sure you'll be a great addition to the team." "Who are you?" The girl with Thomas blurts out, and I could tell there is bitterness in the question. "Oh Jessica, this is…" and he hesitates, waiting for me to fill in the blank. "Sarah," I reply while offering my hand out for a shake, but instead she looks me up and down. "Oh" is all she says. "Well I guess I'll leave you two to your shopping" I say, stepping back and giving them an awkward wave. "See you around Sarah" Thomas says. They walk past me and I look over my shoulder as I watch them walk off. I felt humiliated but angry at the same time. I just made myself look like a fool. He can't have a girlfriend because I'm his girlfriend, right? At least that's what my mind convinced me to believe. How could he even like her? Jake's mom thought I looked like a barbie doll, she should see this girl. I wanted to cry so I make my way under the dock.

After a couple minutes of silence Jason appears. "I thought I'd find you down here." "Sorry, I just didn't feel like being up there anymore." "That bad of a first day?" "No, work was good." "Then, what's wrong?" He asks, plopping down in the sand next to me. " I ran in to Thomas, but he was with some girl." "So?" I give him a glare. "Okay, okay, sorry. I know you have some weird crush on him or whatever it is that causes you girls to get googly-eyed over guys, but it's probably just a fling. I've seen him go through six girlfriends and I've only been here for six months. That's a girlfriend a month! Maybe you can be Miss August?" He says while giving me a playful nudge. I give him another glare, "not cool" "I'm kidding geez." I give him a smirk and just shake my head. "So what did you wanna do?" He asks. "Well I brought some soccer stuff. I was hoping you would practice with me?" "You're actually gonna try out?" "Yeah, I mean why not? It'll give me and you something to do." "Me?" he questions with a puzzled expression. "Come on I need at least one person rooting for me" I say jokingly. He flashes his ever so contagious smile, "Oh, right, number one fan right here."

After about an hour of practicing, I could tell Jason was a little out of shape and was ready for a well needed break. He actually isn't too bad at soccer and gave me some pretty good practice. "How come you don't try out for soccer?" I ask him. "Ah no thanks, I prefer the American version." "Then why don't you try out for the football team?" A disappointing look comes across his face, "I injured my shoulder pretty bad and the doctor advised me that if I wanted to keep the functioning of my arm, it would be best if I didn't play anymore." "I'm so sorry, that's terrible." I tell him. It made me think of all the Friday's I stood in the bleachers cheering for Jake, watching him do what he loved. Jason wasn't the only one that got football taken away from him, but at least Jason's was his own doing and not because his girlfriend wanted to be reckless and selfish. He breaks the silence, "it's alright, it gives me a chance to focus on school and figure out what I want to do with my life I guess." "Well you're not the only one. Since my ex died I haven't been able to move on, he was everything to me and now that he's gone I feel like I'm stuck in limbo not knowing what to do anymore." "That's awful" he murmurs. We both sit there in an awkward silence making it evident we share a mutual despair for each other. "I think we can call it a day, you gave me a pretty good run for my money so looks like I'll be recruiting you for more practice." I say, trying to get rid of the gloomy atmosphere. "Sure thing, anything I can do to help I will. It's getting late though so I should start heading home" he says. "Good idea." We pack

up my stuff and load it into my car and go our separate ways. I sit in my
car checking all my missed notifications. I have a voicemail from Haley,
asking how I am doing and pleading for me to call her. I've been ignoring everyone's calls from home because, let's be honest, I did hold a
slight grudge for the way they went about the whole sending me away
thing. I guess it was time for me to get over myself, I could at least call
my sister, it's not like she had much say in the decision. I finish checking
my messages and decide to call her once I get back to the house.

As I pull out and make my way down the street I spot Jason walking down the road. I feel bad that I didn't offer him a ride. I didn't know
he didn't have a car. "Hey stranger, want a ride?" I ask Jason. "No
thanks, I'm good." "It's not a problem, not like I'm gonna kidnap you or
anything" I say, giving a slight laugh. "Why would you say that" he
snaps, "I said its fine, really." "Damn, okay I was just trying to be nice
but never mind." I start to roll up my window when he puts his hand in
the way. "Wait, I'm sorry. I didn't mean to be harsh. I'm just not allowed
to get rides from people." "So your parents won't let you get a ride from
a friend?" "It's complicated" is all he says. "Alrighty…well I'll talk to

you later then. Let me know when you make it home safe." He gives me a nod and steps back from the car. I shake my head in disbelief as I drive off. Jason's parents must have some serious issues if they are still controlling who he can or can't get a ride from. Oh well, not my problem.

When I get home I have to inform my grandparents on how my first day of work went and of course they think it is the greatest news they ever heard. Got to love grandparents, they take pride in everything you do whether it be minute or monumental. When I finish my dinner I excuse myself and tell them I am going to call Haley. Once I get to my room a wave of uneasiness comes over me. Why do I feel so nervous to call my sister? Probably because this conversation could go one of two ways. Good or bad, and we haven't necessarily gotten along like we use to. Not to mention, I have no clue what to talk about.

"Hello, Sarah, are you there?" "Hey, yeah I'm here." "How are you? You haven't answered or returned any of our calls." "I'm fine, I've just been busy enrolling in school and trying to find a job and all." "Oh, right, well have you done anything fun or seen anything cool?" "Uh, I've gone to the beach a couple times. It's quite a view." "I'm so jealous,

I wish I could trade places with you!" Oh yeah, my life is so peachy because I live close to the ocean. I refrain from being a smart ass and instead tell her how I plan on trying out for the soccer team. "That's great Sarah! I have no doubt that you'll make the team." "Thanks sis, after all I did learn from the best." Haley is the one who got me into soccer. She was the best hands down, it's what she lived for. That's why she received a full ride scholarship. Mom and dad hoped I would follow in her foot steps to ease the costs of college but senior year I decided I liked to party more than anything else. Partying wasn't something I could shake off so easily but the thought of what if still haunts me. "Well I wanted to share what I loved doing with my little sis, I always imagined that one day we would play together in the pros." "And leave it to me to ruin." "Hey don't say that. Soccer isn't for everyone." I debate if I should tell her about Thomas but I quickly decide against it because she would give me a lecture on how I shouldn't pursue soccer for a guy. If I mentioned anything about Thomas, I'm sure she would report to mom and dad right away. "Well I should probably get ready for bed, I have to be up early for work tomorrow. Heaven forbid some brats don't get their frozen yogurt." I tell her. She chuckles, "okay goodnight, love you." "Love you too, grandma and grandpa send their love also." I'm glad I decided to call her, the conversation went pretty well and now it seems as if I did my due diligence. Moments later I get a text from Jason telling me he made it home, now I can go to sleep in peace.

The next morning I am almost late to work thanks to the wonderful LA traffic. It makes me regret all the times I complained about traffic back home. The other drivers here are crazy and rude. When I arrive, Stacy is her chipper self. "Hey Sarah, I got you a coffee. I didn't know how you liked it so I brought all the different sugars and creamers, they had" "Well thanks Stacy, you didn't have to do that though." "Oh it's my pleasure! I don't have very many friends here and not a lot of people are nice to me so it's my way of saying thanks for tolerating me." She gives a slight reassuring laugh. "That's hard to believe, you seem like such a nice girl" I tell her which prompts a big grin from her. "Well thanks! Shall we get everything ready to open.?"

A few hours after we open I run into my first difficult customer. The guy is mad we are out of stock of the only flavor he likes and finds it absolutely absurd that we could forget to order more of the 'only good flavor worth coming to the store' for and it is my fault for being so irresponsible. Luckily Stacy handles it and explains it is actually the shipping companies fault since it was supposed to be here yesterday and they still have yet to deliver it. The guy calmed down and apologized for yelling at me and just leaves, serves him right. Zero points angry customer, one point Sarah and Stacy. I try to avoid confrontational situations because, after the accident I had enough of them with Ms. Henson, that I started having panic attacks when the situation got bad enough. An hour or so later I am cleaning up a spill when I hear a familiar voice over my shoulder.

"Excuse me ma'am, I believe you missed a spot." I look up and see Jason standing there with a sly grin on his face. "Ha ha, very funny, what are you doing here?" I ask him. "What a guy can't get some frozen yogurt?" "Well I mean…" "Chill, ha get it 'cause it's frozen yogurt?" I give him a smile and roll my eyes. "Gee tough crowd. Anyways, I am on break and was wondering when you went on yours?" "Uh, well I'm not sure exactly" I say as I glance over at Stacy. She must've of thought I needed her help again because she makes her way over to us.

"Hi, is there something I can help you with?" Stacy asks. "Why actually yes there is. I was going to see when your coworker here was able to go on break?" "Jason!" "Oh it's okay Sarah, if you want to go a little early I can lock it up for lunch since it's about time anyway." "Are you sure?" "Yeah go ahead, it's no biggie." "Alright, well thanks." I turn to Jason "Let me just go put this stuff away real quick." When I come back from the storage closet I notice Jason and Stacy hitting it off well. As I approach them Stacy is laughing so hard that she lets out a snort. "Oh my gosh, he is hilarious, where did you find him?" "It's a funny story actually" Jason says while looking over at me. "I was in the scuba shop he works at looking around but I guess they were supposed to be closed when bam he runs me over on his skateboard." Stacy's jaw drops. "Which reminds me, why would you ride your skateboard into the shop?" I ask. "If you must know, I'm still learning how to ride the damn thing and I didn't know how to stop myself. Luckily you were there to break my fall" he says, giving me a wink. "Wow, sounds like a keeper"

Stacy chuckles. "Oh, no, it's not like that" I say as I look at Jason. "We aren't together" he adds as he gives me a half smile. "Woops, my bad, I hope I didn't make it awkward" Stacy says. "It's all good" Jason tells her, "but we better get going because I have 45 minutes till I have to get back." "Sarah try to be back around 2:30, that'll give you about an hour." "You got it, thanks Stacy."

"Sorry I didn't mean to give her that impression" Jason says once we make it out the door. "It's okay. Guess it's a rare sight to see a girl and a guy as friends now days." He gives a slight laugh, "yeah I guess so." As we are waiting in line to get some food my phone starts to ring. It's my mom. "Are you gonna get that?" Jason asks. "No I don't feel like arguing right now." While we sit and eat our food we discuss each others likes and dislikes. He is sweet, funny, and caring. Him and Jake would've been good friends. When Jason's break is over I decide to head back to work early since Stacy let me go early. I find Stacy sitting at table not far from where we sat, eating a lunch she brought from home.

"Hi" I say as I approach her. "Oh hey Sarah." " I finished lunch a little early and figured I could open the store back up for you since you were kind enough to let me go early." "Well if you insist but you don't have to." "It's okay, I don't mind" I say giving her a genuine smile. "Alright, it's this key right here" she says as she hands me the ring of keys. "I shouldn't be much longer." "Take your time" I say as I take the keys.

When I make it to the shop, I can't believe who is standing at the door waiting. It's Thomas. Okay, be cool I tell myself. "Hey you." You? Smooth Sarah. "Hey" he says giving me a big smile, "I didn't know you worked here." "Yep, I just started yesterday." "Wow, second day, well I promise not to be that difficult of a customer." "That difficult?" I question, as I open the door to let us both in. "Well yeah, everyone knows you have to give a pretty girl a hard time" he says giving me a wink. That's the second time he's called me pretty, surely that means he likes me. I blush, "Lucky me then" I say. Thomas looks over each flavor before he makes his cup of frozen yogurt and then brings it over to me to weigh. "That'll be $5.45" I state. "What? I don't get a special discount?" Thomas says jokingly. "Nope, sorry, good looks don't pay for everything." Oh my gosh, did I really just say that? He laughs "dang, alright fine." He pulls out a ten dollar bill and hands it to me. "How about instead of a discount, you agree to go on a date with me." "What?" I ask surprised. "You know, like me and you go do something together." I hesitate to answer, I brought this on myself and now I don't even know if I'm ready for it. My heart is clinging on to Jake and even though my mind has me convinced that being with Thomas was like being with Jake, I still felt like a traitor. I love Jake but Jake is dead. "It can be just as friends if you want?" Thomas says as he becomes uneasy due to my hesitation. "What about your girlfriend?" I ask him. "Me and Jessica aren't actually dating. Besides, I know when I see something worth way more." "Oh." "So what do you say?" he asks. "Um, yeah sure" I try to say reassuringly. He grabs the pen off the register and writes his number on the back of his receipt and hands it to me. "Call or text me when you get off". "Okay" I say as I take the receipt from him and starts to walk off, "what about your change?" "That's your tip" he says, giving me another wink as he walks out the door. Once he leaves I just stare at the paper with his number on it. What did I get myself into? Then the door chimes, bringing me back to reality. Thank goodness it was just Stacy.

"I know you just got back but do you mind watching the floor while I go to the bathroom for a minute?" "No problem. Are you feeling okay, you look a little pale?" "I think I may have ate something that didn't sit too well." Another lie of course. "Oh no, well there's some medicine in the back if you think it might help." "Thanks."

I shut the bathroom door and slide down to the floor and start to cry. "I'm sorry Jake, please forgive me." Being in love can be the best feeling in the world but it can also be the most painful. I let a few minutes pass before I get up and splash some cold water on my face so no one could tell I had been crying. For the rest of my shift I just go through the motions. When it comes time to close I let Stacy watch me go through the process. When I get done, she tells me she thinks I will do great on my own. "Meet me tomorrow so you can get your own set of keys" she tells me. We then walk to our cars and as I watch her drive off, I sit in my car pondering over what happened today. I pull my phone out and start looking through pictures of me and Jake. I'm not sure how long I was sitting there before I become startled by a knock on my passenger window.

"Gah Jason, you scared me." I say rolling down the window. "Sorry, I didn't know how else to get your attention. I was just making sure you were okay and not having car trouble." "Oh, no the car is fine, I just needed some time to myself." "Is everything okay?" "No" I reply as I choke back tears. "Woah, hey, Sarah what's wrong?" He goes around to the passenger side and gets in. "Thomas asked me out today." "Wait, what?" He gives me a confused look "I thought that's what you wanted?" "I thought so too, but I don't know if I'm ready." "Well what did you tell him?" "I said yes and now he's expecting me to call him tonight." "You don't have to Sarah, if you need more time you shouldn't rush yourself." "But I need to, I have to at some point." I couldn't hold it back any longer. I let the tears fall as I rest my head on his shoulder while we sit there in silence. After what felt like forever, Jason slips his shoulder out from under me and pulls me into a hug. "Listen to your heart" he whispers and kisses me on the forehead before getting out of the car. "Drive safe and let me know when you make it home" he says as he shuts the door and starts his journey home. I wipe away my tears and drive home.

When I get home, everyone is tucked away for the night, which is a relief because I wouldn't be able to handle my grandparents asking a thousand questions right now. I go to my room and pull out the receipt with Thomas's number scribbled on it and lay it on my nightstand. I begin to pace back and forth, going over what to even say. I finally grab the piece of paper and dial the number. I close my eyes and press the call button. I put the phone up to my ear, one ring, two rings. Maybe he won't answer I think to myself.

"Hello." Shit he answered. "Hellooo" Thomas says again. "Hi Thomas, it's Sarah." "Oh hey beautiful, I was starting to think you weren't gonna call." "Sorry, I got off a little late and I had some things to do when I got home." "No need to apologize. I'm just glad you actually called." "Well why wouldn't I?" "Hey, how do I know you weren't lying just to get me to shut up" he chuckles. "I'm not that mean" I reply. "That mean?" "Well yeah, everyone knows you can't be nice to a guy because he's good looking" I tell him. "You think you're funny huh? Using my words against me." "Maybe just a little" I tell him and it becomes silent. "So, let's get down to business. Where would you like to go?" "I don't know. I'm not sure what all there is around here." "Well what do you like to do for fun?" He asks. "To tell you the truth I'm a pretty boring person, I don't do much." "Oh please" he says, "I bet you are a very interesting person." "I guess you'll just have to find out yourself" I reply. "Would you want to go down to the beach, maybe catch a swim?" The truth is I would have loved that, but I shutter at the thought of him seeing me in a bikini. He would either, never want to look at me again or gawk at me like I was zoo animal. "If you don't mind I would honestly enjoy a little one on one soccer practice with you since I haven't played in awhile." "That sounds fun, when would you like to meet up?" Geez this conversation is taking an eternity. "Uh, how about tomorrow? I get off early since it is Sunday." "Great, it's a date then, I'll just meet you down there?" "Yeah that works." "Awesome, I can't wait! I better let you get some sleep though since it's getting late, but I am so glad you called. It's the perfect way to end my night" he says, making me smile. "Talk to you tomorrow" I tell him. "Goodnight Sarah." "Goodnight Thomas."

Well that didn't go too bad, but my heart still hurts at the thought of betraying Jake. It's okay I tell myself. Thomas is Jake, I mean just look at him. I couldn't fool myself though, Jake's looks isn't what made me fall for him, it was his personality and no one would be able to compare to it. I lay in bed staring at the ceiling fan as it spins around and around. Next thing I know my alarm clock is screaming at me to get up. I get up and start getting dressed when my phone buzzes. It's Thomas.

Good morning, can't wait to see you later. How sweet of him. *Good morning, I'd be lying if I said I wasn't excited to see you either.* I finish getting dressed and make my way down stairs. "Hi, grandma." "Well hello dear, up early aren't you?" "I have to head into work for a bit and if I don't leave early enough the traffic will make me late." "Already getting used to it she says" while letting out a chuckle, "well don't let me stop you, have a good day."

Stacy is overly excited when I make it in to work as she presents me with my own set of keys to Frozen Swirls. "Here ya go, you're officially official girl!" She hands me my keys and turns to walk out the door. "Where are you going?" I ask curiously since technically this was her shift to work. "Oh, um, well if you haven't noticed, it's just kinda me and you here and before you came a long it was just me. I haven't had an actual off day in 2 months. I was hoping once they hired more help I could get some time off." "Oh my gosh, that has got to be illegal." "It's okay, having money has been nice. I can stay if you need me to?" "No, absolutely not. I think I can handle it" I tell her. "Okay, thanks a lot. Call if you need anything."

After she leaves, I don't have a single customer until the lunch crowd shows up and I am pleasantly surprised with how well I do. I never saw myself as a customer service type person but it's not too bad. Luckily nothing too crazy happens. As it gets closer to seven, the more nervous I get. One, it was my first time closing on my own and I did not want to screw it up. Secondly, it was just that much closer till my date with Thomas.

Once I lock up and get everything squared away I go to the bathroom to change. You'd think for picking a date that consisted of working out it would make things less stressful, but that is not the case. I stand in front of the mirror tucking my shirt into my shorts and untucking it at least a dozen time. I finally decide to leave it untucked and emerge from the bathroom and I already see Thomas waiting outside of the shop. Just breathe I tell myself, Jake would want you happy. It's time to start moving on.

"Hey you." Thomas says, giving me a big grin when I come out of the shop. "Hi, sorry it was my first time locking up and I wanted to make sure I did everything right." "You don't have to apologize. I already waited all day, what's another 15 minutes as long as I get to see you." "Oh…" I couldn't help but blush, "that's sweet of you to say." "Shall we?" He says as he sticks his arm out for me to loop my arm around. When we make it to the field, we practice for a good hour before we call it quits. "Whew, you sure gave me a run for my money." Thomas says as he collapses on the ground. "So you think I have a shot?" "A shot? Sarah, I think you have a solid spot on the team." "Thanks, it's just been a couple years and I don't want to embarrass myself." "You have nothing to worry about. The coach will be begging you to join." We laid in the field for two hours, opening up to one another about who we are, what are dreams are, and the interests and disagreements we share. Of course I didn't tell him about Jake, but I might one day. For now I 'll trust Jason with that secret. I enjoyed my time with Thomas and I was actually disappointed when our date came to an end but I knew I'd be hating myself in the morning when I had to get ready for work. He walks me to my car where we just stare at one another awkwardly for a couple seconds. "Well I had an amazing time Sarah. You seem like a genuine girl and I hope you'll let me take you out again." "Thank you Thomas, I really enjoyed tonight too." "The pleasure was all mine…" he kisses my hand. "Text me when you make it home." "I will" I tell him. On the way home, I replay the night's events over in my head. When I make it home I text Thomas like I promised and just as I am getting ready for bed I get a text from Jason.

How'd your date with Thomas go?

We hit it off really well, I enjoyed myself for the first time in a long time.

Dang, I must be chopped liver then.

Shut up, you know what I mean, go to bed cry baby!

Fine. Talk to you tomorrow?

Duh.

Chapter 5

It is finally August and school starts in two days. I couldn't help but feel anxious about getting back out into the social realm but Jason has been a great friend and has really helped calm my nerves. We have managed to hang out at least every other day since we've met. Thomas left the day after our first date for a last minute trip with his parents. He offered me to go with them, but I felt like that would have been too awkward. However, that hasn't stopped him from texting me non-stop. I can feel myself starting to have feelings for Thomas but something seems to be holding me back from truly opening up my heart. Is it my deep rooted feelings for Jake or just my own personal reservations? I can't tell.

"Are you nervous to start school" Jason asks. "Well yeah. New place, new school, new people. Not exactly the best situation for a someone with depression and anxiety" I tell him. "Touché, but at least you have me" he says, giving me his big pearly grin. "This is true. I'm so glad we met each other. Speaking of, today is our two-month friendaversary." "Our what?" he asks while letting out laugh. "Our anniversary of friendship for knowing each other for two months" I reply. "Well I didn't get you a gift, what did you get me?" "Uh, my friendship" I say. We both laugh. "Seriously though, thank you for being such a great friend. I feel like I've known you forever" I tell him. "Same here. I feel like we've had this instant connection since we met. I was such a loner, new to the city and no one to lean on till you came around" he says and then takes my hands in his, "Sarah I have to tell you something." Before he can say another word a loud ring interrupts him. "Oh sorry" I say as I pull out my phone, "it's Thomas." "Go ahead" Jason says. "I'll be quick and then you can tell me what you were gonna say." He nods.

I walk off a little ways before answering. "Hey Thomas." "Hi beautiful, what are you doing?" "Just down at the beach hanging out with Jason." "Ah you sure know how to make a man jealous. What if I told you I was on the way home from the air-port?" Thomas says "Are you really?" "Yep. What do you say, can I see you?" "Yeah, I'd like that" I tell him. "Great I'll see you soon then." "Alright."

I make my way back over to Jason. "What did lover boy have to say?" Jason teases. "He's back from his trip and asked if he could see me." Oh, cool" Jason says. "I told him he could meet us here." "Us?" "Uh yeah, I want my best-friend to know the guy I am potentially going to date." "I don't know Sarah. I think he probably just wants it to be you and him. I'll let you two have some time to yourselves. I'll talk to you later though" he says as he gets up to leave. "Wait, what were you gonna say before he called?" He pauses, "I'll have to tell you when we have more time" he says before continuing his way up the hill.

After Jason leaves, I sit there thinking about what he could have wanted to tell me. I mean I'm not a dummy. He could've been about to confess that he has feelings for me. However, anxiety has its way of making you question the simplest of things. What if it was something else, there is something off about him after all. My thoughts are interrupted by a tap on my shoulder. As I look up, I see Thomas staring back down at me, grinning from ear to ear. As I stand up, Thomas reveals flowers that were hidden behind his back. "These are for you." "Thank you, you are so sweet" I say as I take the flowers. "Where's Jason?" "He left not too long ago." "Oh. Well hey now we can make it a date" he says before continuing, "would you like to get some dinner? I am starving." "Sure. I could go for something to eat myself." We make our way up the dock as we discuss where we should eat. We agree on a pizza joint just a couple buildings down from where I work. As we walk past Frozen Swirls I glance in to see how busy work is tonight. There are no customers. Instead I see Jason and Stacy sitting at the yogurt bar and they appear to be laughing hysterically as Stacy rests her hand on Jasons thigh. I look away quickly and couldn't help but feel a little jealous. Am I hurt because Jason is getting close with someone else or did I have feelings for Jason too? Maybe he was trying to tell me that he is interested in Stacy. Paranoid that Thomas might actually hear what I was thinking, I glance over at him. Luckily, he is distracted by some guys playing soccer in the distance. "Are those more guys from school?" I ask. "Nah, they are from another school, they're pretty good." "Not as good as you though" I say, giving him a playful nudge. He smiles and puts his arm around me.

Once we arrive to the pizza place we take our seat and order a pepperoni pizza to share. We discuss his trip and then everything I had done while he was away. "Oh, I almost forgot" he says while checking all of his pockets before he pulls out a bracelet. "I got this for you, while I was in Costa Rica." "Thomas that is so sweet, you didn't have to do that." "Of course I did. Mind if I put it on you?" I hold out my arm. As he ties it around my wrist, I admire the braided twine and single bright pink stone heart attached to it. "Thank you, it's so pretty" "Just like you" Thomas says. I had to resist the urge to cry. The sweeter Thomas is to me and the closer we become, the more I miss Jake. What is wrong with me. I am obsessing over my dead ex-boyfriend who would only want me to be happy. If that is true then why do I feel so guilty? Probably because it's my fault he is dead, yet, I get to go on with my life. Thomas notices my silence, "Is everything okay?" He asks. "Yeah sorry, just a little distracted is all." "Wanna talk about it?" I hesitate, debating if I should tell him. It would probably be better to tell him sooner rather than later. I decide against my better judgement that I should tell him. I take a deep breath to muster up the courage and begin my story.

"Wow." Is all he says once I finish. I start to panic on the inside, instantly regretting that I told him. He grabs my hands, "I had no idea, that is a tough situation to go through and I am sorry if I have pressured you in any way. We can slow things down if you'd like and I want you to know I will always be here for you if you need me." I let the tears fall. It felt good to finally tell someone. I haven't even told Jason the full story, not because I didn't trust him, but because of how early on he asked in our friendship. "Hey, you're okay" Thomas reassures me, as he uses his thumb to wipe away the tears on my cheek. "Thank you" I mumble. The embarrassment starts to settle once I realize I am attracting stares. Thomas must have read my mind because he stands up and motions for me to grab his hand. "Let's get out of here." "Good idea" I say as I take his hand.

Chapter 6

"So, you told him about your ex?" Jason asks. "Yeah, well except the fact that he looks identical to him." "How did he take it?" "Surprisingly well, he was really nice about it. I think it actually brought us closer." "Oh" Jason replies as he directs his gaze at the ground, "well, that's good I guess." "Speaking of close, I didn't know you and Stacy have been hitting it off so well." Jason's face turns red, "We were just talking. She saw me walking by and called my over." "Hey, no need to explain, I was just saying" I tell him. "She's not even my type" he says defensively. "Oh is that so? I didn't know you had a type." He lets out a small laugh, "everyone's got a type Sarah. For instance, Thomas is your type." For some reason his words stung a little more than they should have. I never considered myself to be superficial and like a certain type, but then again, here I am interested in a guy who looks just like my ex, so I guess that would indeed be a type. "Well what's your type then?" I ask sarcastically. "That's for me to know and for you to find out" he says, giving me his charming smile. What is that supposed to mean? Does Jason have a girlfriend already? Surely, he would've introduced us by now. Besides, would she be okay with her boyfriend hanging out with some girl this whole time? "Come on, your next class is in 15 minutes, I don't want you to be late on your first day" he says, interrupting my thoughts.

My first day back in school hasn't been that bad, but people aren't kidding when they say it's hard to get back into the swing of school once you've been out of it awhile. It helps having Business Communications as my first class every Monday and Wednesday. It's the class me and Jason have together and we each have a break before our next class. I think Jason being here has helped keep my anxiety from going into over drive and has given me the confidence to go about my day. Today also happens to be try outs, but they aren't until five. I'll get out of my second and last class of the day at three so I'll have two hours to spare. It makes me want to vomit just thinking about it.

As I get out of my last class I get a text from Thomas.

Men's try outs are gonna be at the South field, so looks like I won't get to see you try out after all): I know you are going to kick ass though! Good luck gorgeous (:

Ugh, I was hoping you could be there, I am nervous. I would wish you luck, but you don't need it, captain.

Man that sucks. I was really hoping Thomas could be there. Jake never got to watch me play because football always conflicted, that is, until I quit playing. At least I'll have Jason there to help ease my nerves. I decide to eat a light lunch so there's not a chance of me throwing it up during try outs. After lunch I do some reading to get ahead in class. As 4:30 rolls around I get a text from Jason.

Hey, so looks like my lab is going to run late so I won't be there at the start. I am really sorry. You are going to do great though, I believe in you!!

Noooo. First Thomas, now you too. Whose stupid idea was it to try out.

Yours remember… and it's not stupid. You're going to make the team and I will be there as soon as I can. Deep breath, you got this!

Welp, there goes the only two people in my support group. I walk to my car and grab my soccer bag and start to head to the locker room.

As I put my hair into a ponytail, I could feel my nerves growing as my palms start to sweat. Once I finish getting changed, I make my way to the field and there's about 30 girls out here to try out.

"Attention, ladies I am Coach Johnson we will be starting try outs in five minutes. If you could please form two lines and write your name and the position you're interested in. We will split you up according to positions to run some drills while another group will be scrimmaging. After about 30 minutes the groups will switch. This way we can assess your abilities as individuals and as a team. The roster will be posted tomorrow on my door, so do not pester me for an answer. Best of luck to you all."

I get in line and list my desired position as midfielder and my alternate position as a forward. I don't think I am a very good forward but it's the only other position I don't mind playing and the more positions you can play the greater the odds of making the team. After everyone signs in, they split us in to two groups. I end up in group one, which means I'll be running drills first. As everyone is splitting up, I get shoulder chucked by someone going the opposite way.

"Oops. Guess I didn't see you there Susie." As I turn around it's, Jess, the girl I had seen Thomas with on the dock. "Oh, um it's Sarah." "Same difference" she says as she smirks and walks off. Great, the last thing I need is some drama in my life, at least she isn't in my group.

After 30 minutes they blow the whistle for a water break and we switch stations. As I make my way to the water buffalo I spot Jason in the bleachers waving frantically. I give him a wave back and he smiles while giving me a thumbs up. Knowing Jason is here supporting me gives me the confidence boost I need going into the scrimmage portion. At first they start me out as a midfielder but there are so many trying out for the position that they move me to a forward. I score two points and another girl scores three, allowing our side to win. By time it is over with I have mixed emotions over my performance. I feel like I did well, but then again I have no clue how I compare to the others. The only thing I have going for me is there aren't as many trying out for the forward position.

"Sarah you killed it out there!" Jason exclaims as he puts his hands up for a double high five. "Thanks" I reply as I high five him, "I am so nervous though. I wish tomorrow would hurry up so I can know already." "Great, you're going to be a nervous wreck until you find out, aren't you?" "You got that right." "So, what's the plan? Pre-celebratory dinner for the newest Spartans soccer player?" "Don't you think that would jinx it?" "Oh please, if only you could see the way they were watching you and would mark their clipboards when you made a play." "What? Oh, don't tell me that" I groan.

"Hey how'd it go?" I hear from behind, and I turn to see Thomas jogging up. "Hey Thomas. It went okay, I think" I tell him. "Psh, okay," Jason scoffs "she looked like a pro. I told her she has nothing to worry about." "Well I am gonna take Jason's word for it, because I know you're too hard on yourself." "You can say that again" Jason says as he rolls his eyes. "Hey what is this, gang up on Sarah time?" Thomas laughs, "Not at all, in fact, I was curious what we are going to do to celebrate?" "Well Jason had mentioned getting dinner, I'm sure we are all starving. I could hardly eat beforehand." "Oh" Thomas says, "I was hoping to take you out for a little one on one time, but, that's cool too, the more the merrier!" "Actually" Jason interrupts, "it's okay, you two can go ahead. I'll spare myself the third wheel awkwardness." "What, Jason don't be ridiculous, it was your idea to begin with" I say, glancing at Thomas for support. "Yeah, dude it's not a problem" Thomas adds. "Ah it's okay. I already got homework I need to get a jump start on. You two have fun though, I'll catch ya tomorrow Sarah" Jason says as he gives us wave and walks off. It sucks watching him walk off. The closer I got to Jason the less I wanted to be away from him. "Ready to go?" Thomas asks as he kisses my hand. "Yeah" I say as reach down to grab my bag and I notice Jess in the distance glaring at us. I quickly look away to avoid eye contact. What is she still doing here? I hope she isn't trying to start any drama because she thinks I stole Thomas from her. It was his own doing. As we make our way to the car, I gather the courage to ask him about it.

"Why did you break up with Jess?" I ask Thomas. "I told you, I know when I recognize something worth more than just a stupid fling" Thomas says with a smile as he grabs a hold of my hand. "Yeah but how do you know I'm not just a stupid fling. There are a lot of pretty girls at this school. What if you decide I'm just a stupid fling, then what? Adios

Sarah?" "Look," he stops walking and looks me in the eyes, "I know my track record isn't the best but I don't want my past mistakes to make you doubt the awesome connection we have. And, if we are being honest I have been waiting for the right time to ask you to be my girlfriend. I know you've gone through a lot and that's why I wanted to take things slow. I've seen a lot of girls, there's no denying that but I've never asked any of them to be my girlfriend" He stops talking and is now waiting for a response. I did not expect this, and now I have no idea how to respond. "But why me?" I ask, feeling the lump in my throat form. "Because," he says as he steps closer to me, "from the moment I met you laying on that field, I became mesmerized by how beautiful you are and now that I've gotten to know you, I've realized you're not like other girls. You're special Sarah." I look away. I am undeserving of his affection and the longer I look into his eyes the more it makes me miss Jake. Am I capable of loving someone the way I did Jake? How would I know unless I tried? Thomas gently turns my head to face his and now we are face to face and my heart feels like it is about jump out of my chest. He embraces my head between his hands and presses his soft lips to mine.

When he pulls away he looks me in the eyes and asks, "so what do you say?" "To what?" "Will you be my girlfriend?" Staring into his eyes is like a trap that I can't escape from. I simply nod and give him the best smile I could muster. Thomas gives me a big smile and picks me up and twirls me around before he puts me back down. "Then lets go eat, girl-friend."

The next morning Thomas offers to pick me up for school so we can check the roster together. I quickly agree, but should have known there would be a catch. Thomas wants me to meet his parents after school today. Needless to say, I am going to be a nervous wreck all day.

"Sarah, there's a handsome young man at the door for you" my grandma calls from downstairs. Ugh, I told him to wait outside. I hurry and grab my bag and rush downstairs. As I'm making my way down, I see Thomas and my grandma talking. "Hey, sorry, I was running behind" I tell Thomas. "You're fine, it's just raining like crazy out there and I didn't want you to get soaked" he says as he holds up his umbrella. "Oh dear, what a gentleman" grandma exclaims as she gives me a devious side eye. I give a nervous laugh and realize the proper thing to do is in-

troduce them. "Grandma, this is Thomas, my fr..boyfriend, he plays soccer too. Thomas this my grandma." "Well Mrs. Caldwell it is very nice
to finally meet you" he says as he gives my grandma a kiss on the hand.
Her giggle lets me know she is flattered. I wonder where grandpa is in
hopes of avoiding the formalities for another time, but I am anxious to
get to school to see if I made the team. "Grandma keep your fingers
crossed, I find out if I made the team today." "Oh pish posh, Sarah. You
know you did, now you two better get going, traffic is going to be hor-
rendous in this weather." "Thanks grandma, see you later" I say. As we
turn to leave, grandma grabs Thomas by the elbow and looks him direct-
ly in the eyes, "Please drive careful, life is precious." She looks at me
and I instantly get goosebumps. I know she is referring to that night and
I can't help but feel my heart drop into my stomach. Thomas gives her a
nod, "Yes ma'am" he replies.

Once we arrive outside coach Johnson's office I start scanning the
list. "Oh my God, I did it, I made the team!" I turn towards Thomas,
beaming with pride. "Atta girl! I knew you would" he says as he plants a
kiss on me. "What position?" "Forward, but that's okay, I probably

wouldn't have gotten much playing time as a midfielder anyway." "Well you're going to be great regardless, babe" I smile and tell him thanks. I would be lying if I said him calling me babe didn't throw me off a little bit, but I guess I need to get use to the whole dating thing again. My next thought is that I can't wait to tell Jason I made the team. I wonder when he gets out of his first class, so I send him a text.

Hey! When do you get out of class, I got good news!

Sorry I won't be at school today but hmm…let's see, does it have anything to do with the fact that you made the team!?

Are you okay?? Yes, you are looking at one of Pacific's newest forwards!

Yeah, I'm fine. Figured I didn't want to show up to school soaking wet. That's great though, I am so happy for you, I knew you could do it!

I feel so bad. I forgot that Jason doesn't drive so with it raining today I don't blame him for missing school. As 10:00 approaches, me and Thomas part our ways for class. Shortly after I get out of my second class, I get another text from Jason.

Think we can hang out later?

I am going to meet Thomas' parents here shortly but maybe after-wards?

Wow, sounds like things are getting pretty serious between you two. I don't wanna intrude, I'll see you tomorrow in class?

You bet!

If only he knew. I don't know why but part of me didn't want to tell him that Thomas and I are a couple now. What if it changes things between us? It was going to come out one way or another though and the best thing to do would be to tell him myself. I'll tell him tomorrow when I see him.

I make my way to the parking lot and Thomas is already at his car chatting with two of his teammates. As I approach them, I recognize Randy from the very first encounter with Thomas at the field.

"Hey, I remember you" Randy says. I laugh, "yeah I remember you too." "That's good that means no amnesia for you."

"Hey babe," Thomas says as he sticks his hand out for me to grab. "Guys this is my girlfriend, Sarah. Sarah, this is Randy and Ian." "Hi there" I say as I give them both a wave. "Nice to meet the lady behind the name" Ian says. "Well we'll catch ya later dude." Randy says as him and Ian give Thomas a special handshake. "Alright, later guys." Thomas says and then turns to me with a big a smile, "you ready?" "Ready as I'll ever be, I guess" I tell him. He comes around and opens the door for me, "oh, come on, it won't be that bad, they've been dying to meet you."

When we pull up to his house, it was just as I figured. A big luxurious gated house with palm trees lining the drive way. When Thomas told me, his dad is a lawyer and his mom is a plastic surgeon I assumed they would be well off, and my judgement was correct. When we enter the house, we are greeted by a barking dog. Thomas bends down to pet the dog, "Hey there buddy, have you been a good boy?" The dog quits barking once he's received his proper hello and then moves on to sniff the stranger that is in his home. "This is Max." "Why hello Max" I say as I bend down for him to sniff my hand. He gives my hand an approving lick before he trots off into the other room.

"Thomas, is that you?" A woman's voice shouts from the other room. "Yes mom, and I have someone I'd like you to meet." An immediate shriek arises from the other room and footsteps start to make their way in our direction. Oh boy here it goes, I think to myself as I pull my hair forward and straighten out my shirt. "Stop it, you look fine" Thomas whispers to me. A beautiful middle-aged woman with long wavy brown hair appears in front of us. "Why hellooo, you must be Sarah" the woman states. "Sarah, this is my mom." "Hi Mrs. Carter, it's nice to meet you" I say as I stick my hand out for a handshake. She ignores my hand and gives me a hug instead, "Oh hun, you can call me Teresa. Now, please come in, make yourself at home." "Where's dad?" Thomas asks. "He should be home any minute, in the mean time can I get you anything to drink Sarah?" "Some water would actually be great" I reply. "You got it!" She disappears, and Thomas and I are left alone sitting in the living room. Thomas looks at me and holds my hand, "we don't have to stay long if you are feeling uncomfortable, I just wanted them to finally meet you." "It's okay, I am just nervous. I don't want them to hate me." "Don't be silly, they are excited, you're the first girl

since high school that I've brought home." "Wow, no pressure or anything" I say as he chuckles and kisses my forehead. "Here you go hun"
Teresa says as she hands me a glass of water. "Thank you very much." A
moment of silence falls as I take a sip of water and I hear footsteps approaching from behind. A deep southern draw breaks the silence, "Hey
everyone, sorry I'm late." I stand up and turn to greet the man speaking.
The man looks like a middle-aged version of Thomas with the exception
of Thomas being a few inches taller than him. "Dad this is Sarah." "Hi
there" he says as he sticks his hand out for a shake "you can call me
David or Dave, whatever you prefer." I shake his hand "nice to meet you
David." "So, what's for dinner?" David asks Teresa while patting his
belly. "I was thinking meatloaf, mashed potatoes, and some green beans"
she replies. "You sure know the way to my heart" he says as he gives her
a kiss, "I'm gonna go change and then I'll be back down." Teresa then
looks at us with a smile "well, I certainly hope you'll stay for dinner
Sarah. We would love to get to know you more." Thomas looks at me
for a response, "I would love to." I say, not wanting disappoint her. "Oh,
wonderful" she exclaims while clapping her hands together, "I'll go get

started." I rise once more and ask if she would like my help. She denies and insists I just relax.

After dinner we all make ourselves cozy in the living room to play some cards. Around nine we decide to call it a night. Before retiring to their room, Teresa and David tell me how much they enjoyed my company and that I am welcome over anytime. I guess I made a pretty good first impression after all, and not to mention, I had a genuinely good time. I should probably go to the bathroom before Thomas takes me home so I have him point me the way. On my way to the bathroom, I stop and look at the photos hanging along the wall. I can't help but giggle at the transition of baby Thomas up to middle school brace face Thomas. Next, I come across what appears to be a family photo of David, Teresa, Thomas, and a girl that I don't recognize. I don't remember Thomas telling me he had a sister. I wait till we get in the car to ask him about the girl in the photo.

"So, I saw some of your photos hanging in the hallway." Thomas laughs, "oh yeah? Looks like I didn't get to avoid the embarrassing baby photo sharing after all." "Oh whatever, you were a cutie" "What? You mean to tell me I'm not still a cutie?" Thomas teases. I roll my eyes, "I didn't say that" I pause before continuing. "Do you have a sister?" I can tell the question was a bit unnerving to Thomas' as his smile fades and the grip on his steering wheel gets tighter. "Sorry, I didn't mean to upset you. You don't have to answer that." "No it's okay" he replies before letting out a heavy sigh. "Um, yeah I do. Well, I did. Her name was Emily. She passed away five years ago from cancer." "I'm so sorry Thomas." I look at him and I can see the tears welling up in his eyes. I grab his hand and hold it. "It's not your fault. I should've told you but it's still so hard to accept sometimes." "I understand completely" I say, giving his hand a squeeze. "I know you do" he replies, giving me a half smile. I decide not to make things harder on him, and leave it at that. We ride in silence until we pull up to my grandparents.

"I had a great time with you tonight" Thomas says. I smile at him, "me too, tonight was just what I needed, thank you." He gets out and opens my door for me, and walks me to the front door where we both stop and linger for a moment. He gives me a frown, "I guess it's time for you to go then." "Unfortunately" I reply. He tucks my hair behind my ear and gazes into my eyes for a quick second before giving me a kiss which is immediately interrupted by the opening of the front door. My grandpa clears his throat, making his presence known. We pull away quickly even though we had already been caught. "Um, hello sir." Thomas says nervously as he sticks his hand out for a shake. "My name is Thomas." Grandpa shakes his hand, "Hello Thomas. I hope you're treating our sweet Sarah like a lady should be treated." "Grandpa" I exclaim as I begin to blush. "Yes sir, of course." "Good, that's what I want to hear. Anyways, I was just about to lock up for the night. Don't be too much longer sweet pea" grandpa says as he slowly shuts the door. "Sorry" I mouth to Thomas but he simply wipes his brow and gives me a smile. "Goodnight Sarah." "Goodnight Thomas," I say and then enter the house. Ugh, talk about embarrassing.

I pass by my grandpa on the way to my room. He raises an eyebrow at me when we make eye contact. "Yes, grandpa?" I say. "Oh, nothing" he says letting out a chuckle "just glad to see you settling in well." I give him a teasing side eye, "goodnight grandpa" I say as I give him a kiss on the cheek. "Goodnight dear."

Chapter 7

"Hey, you" Jason says giving me his near perfect smile as he plops in the seat next to mine. "Hey yourself, missed you yesterday" I tell him. "See I knew I was irresistible" he jokes, giving me a wink. I just reply with a laugh, but the thing is there is some truth to it. Jason is quite the charmer and not to mention, easy on the eyes. It's no wonder I enjoy his company so much. "So, what have I missed in the life of Sarah?" "Well I made the team" I beam. "Hell yeah you did. I can't wait to watch you play!" "Really?" "Uh, duh, I wouldn't miss it." "Unless you have a lab that runs late that is" I say teasingly, giving him a nudge. "Hey, give me a break, it was the first day." He laughs, "so how are things between you and Thomas?" There was a part of me that was hesitant to tell him. I couldn't help but feel that if I tell him about Thomas and I, it would change things between us and that's not a risk I am eager to take, but keeping the truth from him would only be worse. "Um, good" I tell him, but, before I can say anything else our professor approaches the podium and clears his throat to gain our attention.

Once class is over, me and Jason head to the food court for some lunch. "I hate to be that guy, but do you think I can borrow your book for class? They've cut my hours at the shop, so I haven't been able to buy all my books yet." "Oh, now I see why you hang out with me" I say sarcastically. "Trust me, that's not it" he says giving me another smile. "Well I suppose so. It's not like I've already read through chapter 14 or anything" I say as I hand him the book. "Overachiever" he scoffs. "Under-achiever" I say teasingly. He cocks his head at me and puts his hands up like he's going to tickle me. I give him a stern look, "don't you dare." He starts to tickle me and I can't help but burst with laughter. "Jake stop it," I manage to choke out as I punch him softly on the shoulder. We both come to a halt at the realization of what I just said. I look away, filled with embarrassment. Jake was the only person who knew I was ticklish so he would tickle me when I got on his nerves. "Gee I'm sorry Sarah" Jason says softly. "It's okay, I don't know what overcame me" I say. "Wanna get some food?" Jason asks, changing the the subject. I nod while still in disbelief that I called Jason, Jake. We grab our food and find a seat in the court yard. "Do you work tonight?" "Not anymore. Stacy asked to switch. I guess she has a birthday party to go to tomorrow or something." "Well if you're up for it, there is a mini carnival going on down by the pier that I was hoping we could go to?" "Sure, that sounds fun." "Great, I'll meet you down there around six?" "Yeah that sounds good" I tell him. I pause to think for a moment. "You know I can give you a ride, right?" "I appreciate it, I just don't think it would be such a good idea if my mom finds out." "No offense Jason, but, I think your mom needs to let loose a little." "Yeah she can be over the top sometimes, but I've put her through a lot so it's the least I could do." "Do you think if you introduced me to her then she might be comfortable with me giving you rides?" "Um, not really" he replies. "Well it's worth a shot, right?" He becomes restless, "Well, she doesn't actually live with me, is the thing" he says. "Then what's the big deal?" "It's complicated and I'd rather not divulge on the subject." "Okay, okay. No rides, got it, but hold on. You mean to tell me that you have your own place and we are always hanging out at my grandparents?" "And I've said too much" Jason says as he looks over both shoulders before continuing, "it's a long story but I am in hiding, but please Sarah, you can't tell anyone this. Promise me?" He gives me a pleading look. "I promise." There has always been something mysteriously alluring about Jason, but for him to be hiding, that is a bit disturbing to hear. He could be in hiding for a number of reasons, but I didn't want to push the subject so I didn't ask any more questions. Fortunately it was time for my next class, so we part our ways.

Afterwards I get the inkling to go shopping so I make a pit stop at a close by strip mall. With everything going on I haven't had any time for myself and it is refreshing to have some time to myself. I find a cute dress that's on sale, a new shirt and a pair of shorts that I buy before I decide to head home. When I get home the house is unusually empty, Hector or Esther aren't even wandering about. I make my way upstairs to change and get ready for tonight. I decide to wear my new dress despite the scar on my thigh peeking out just below the edge of my dress. I figure there's no point in hiding my scars anymore now that I am on the soccer team. To my surprise, no one has asked about it and besides, I feel comfortable enough around Jason that I don't have to hide my true self. Before leaving I make another walk through the house so see if anyone has come home. Still empty. Hmm. Sometimes my grandparents have to travel for their jobs, but, surely, they would have given me a heads up or left a note. If no one's home by time I get back tonight I'll give them a call.

When I arrive, I head to our usual meeting spot. As I approach the underside of the dock I see that Jason is on the phone. I am still too far away to hear what is being said, but the conversation sounds heated. As I get within range I hear Jason tell the person, "I'm done discussing this, this conversation is over" before he hangs up. I stop for a moment so that way he doesn't think I overhead his conversation, but I can't help but wonder who he was talking to and what it was about. I let a few minutes pass before I walk up to him and tap him on the shoulder. When he turns to face me his mouth falls open, but no words come out. I raise an eyebrow and cock my head. "You look beautiful" he finally says, which prompts me to blush. "Thanks" I reply, giving him a bashful smile. "Shall we?" Jason asks as he motions up towards the dock.

As we make our way up to the carnival, we agree to get food first. More like junk food because none of this food is nutritious. We each get a candy apple, I get a small cone of cotton candy, Jason gets a turkey leg, and we share a funnel cake. "Ugh I am stuffed" I say as I pat my belly. "I know, now we just need to ride one of those fast spinning rides so we can throw it back up." "Um no, that's exactly the opposite of what we need to do" I reply. "Fineee. Lets go play some games then." We try our luck at ring toss first, which we both quickly determine that we suck at and move on to find another game. "Oh my gosh look how cute that stuffed raccoon is with the big eyes" I tell him. "Seriously? If you saw that in real life, the is last thing you would be thinking." I roll my eyes and turn to the carnival worker.

"How much to play?" "Five dollars will get you five darts and you have to pop four to win a prize." I hand him five dollars and take the darts. I give it my best shot but I only manage to pop three balloons. "It's rigged" I say turning back around to Jason. He laughs and pulls out his wallet and hands the worker five dollars. Jason pops all four balloons and looks back at me with a smirk. "Pick your prize, any prize" the worker shouts. "I'll take the raccoon." "Really Jason, you don't even like that one." "I don't, but you do" he says as he hands me the raccoon. "My, my Jason aren't you sweet." "Only sometimes" he says giving me a wink. We continue our way through the carnival when suddenly Jason grabs my hand and pulls me the other way, "come on lets ride the Ferris Wheel" he says as he tugs me towards it.

He is so excited and I don't want to ruin it, but truth be told I am afraid of heights. I thought I would have time to gather myself but when we make it to the gate there isn't a line. We were seated right away and it starts rolling up before coming to a jolted stop. I grab Jason's hand. "Jason I'm scared. I have a phobia of heights." He squeezes my hand, "I got you Sarah. I would never let anything happen to you." I can feel myself starting to hyperventilate. "Hey quit looking down. Look up at the sky. Do you see the stars?" Jason says. I do as he says, and I can't help but become mesmerized by the stars. "It's beautiful" I whisper. I look over at Jason and catch him staring at me. "What?" I ask. "I have to tell you something" he says. "Okay…" I say slowly. "Ever since I met you, I can't help but feel whole. I feel like I've known you my whole life, like we share this instant connection. Hell, before I even met you I had dreams about you and when I ran into you that day, I knew you were the girl I had been dreaming about. You are my missing puzzle piece Sarah." "Jason" I say trying to find the right words. "No, let me finish. I've put this off long enough. You are beautiful, strong, funny, and smart. It's no wonder Thomas likes you and I know you're attracted to him but I really like you Sarah and I'm hoping what we have between us is more than just friendship." I swallow hard, trying to get rid of the lump in my throat. He is right but his words are already too late. I am in a relationship with Thomas and I needed to tell Jason now more than ever, but I can't bring myself to do so. I didn't want to ruin this moment of raw emotion. I let go of his hand and push his blonde shaggy hair to the side and stare into his blue eyes. He presses his forehead to mine, causing my heart to beat uncontrollably. I know what's going to happen next and despite knowing how wrong it is, I can't find the will to stop it. He kisses me passionately, triggering a tingly feeling to erupt through my entire body. I lean into him and kiss him back. Jason isn't wrong, being with him feels right, but I can't deny my newly established relationship with Thomas. What did I get myself into, and how am I going to tell Jason about Thomas after he just put his feelings on the line? As we pull away, Jason flashes me his hard to resist smile and I return the smile. "Was that so bad" he asks me. "Huh?" He looks forward indicating that the ride was over. "Oh. Not really." I answer. The ironic part is now I didn't want to get off. Getting off meant it wasn't just me and Jason anymore.

"So, what should we do next?" Jason asks cheerily. "Let's find another ride" I suggest. We start walking aimlessly amongst the crowd trying to find our next source of entertainment. I feel a tap on my shoulder and I turn to see Jess and Randy. "Hello Sarah." "Uh, hey Jess." "I'm curious, since you and Thomas are officially boyfriend and girlfriend now, does he approve of you being on a date with another guy." Jason looks at me and I can see the hurt in his eyes. "It's not a date Jess, but yes Thomas knows I'm here." "Yeah, we're just friends after all" Jason adds, and I can hear the coldness in his tone. Even though Jason is the victim here, I can't help but feel my heart sink to the bottom of my stomach. "Whatever," she flips her hair "just thought I'd ask" she says before walking off. Randy gives an awkward smile before following behind her.

I turn to Jason, "I'm sorry, I've been waiting for the right time to tell you." "Save it Sarah. It doesn't even matter." "Yes, it does." I start to cry. "How could you lead me on like that? Especially after what I just told you" he says angrily. "I'm sorry" I sob. "What? You felt sorry for me or something?" "No! That's not it, it's complicated." "It always is Sarah. Whatever, I'm leaving" he says as he tries to walk off. "Please don't" I beg as I grab his hand. "You made your choice and I have nothing else to say." He breaks my free from grip and I watch him disappear into the crowd. I know better than to follow him, so I head to my car. I know I am too emotionally unstable to drive so I sit in my car until I get my crying under control.

When I pull up to the house I see Hector unloading some bags from the limo. Looks like wherever grandma and grandpa planned on going didn't work out. "Hey Hector, would you like a hand?" "Oh no, that's quite okay miss Sarah, this is the last of it" he says as he pulls out the last two bags. Wait a second. I recognize that bag, it's one of Haley's bags. "Hector who is here?" "Why your parents and sister of course." "What" I exclaim, as my voice rises a little. "I'm sorry Sarah, I thought you knew." "No, I didn't" I mumble. Great. This is the last thing I need right now, and not to mention, the one person that I can vent to doesn't even want to talk to me right now. It's not like I can leave either, Hector already knows I was here and he might say something. I take a couple deep breathes and count to ten before heading in.

"Sarah!" Haley says as she rushes to give me a hug. "Oh my gosh, Haley. What are you doing here?" I say doing my best to act surprised. "Um well" she lowers her voice, "mom is upset you haven't been answering her calls or even tried to call since you've been here, and she told Dr. Loucheski. He suggested that either we make a surprise visit to check on you or he would. I know how much you hate him, so I suggested we all make a family trip down." "She is insane, she was the one who wanted me to leave and now she's worried about me." "Well we all are Sarah" she grabs my hand, "I mean, we talked once, a month ago but that was it." I look away, she's right I've been a bad sister and I'm sure living at home alone with mom and dad hasn't been a walk in the park. "Also..." she gives me an awkward smile before continuing, "grandma called and told us that you have a boyfriend." Dammit. That's exactly why I told him to wait in the car. They are going to expect me to give them all the little mushy details and heaven forbid, want to meet Thomas. "Well, is it true?" Haley, asks, interrupting my thoughts. "Uh, yeah but it's not anything serious though." She gives me a little nudge, "What's his name? Is he a cutie?" "Thomas and uh yeah I guess so." "Ooh, I can't wait to meet him." I muster a chuckle, "yeah I bet," but if there was one thing for sure, they were not going to meet Thomas. If they did, I can already see it now. They will say I am only with him because he looks like Jake and use it as an excuse to put me in the looney bin. At first I admit, his looks caught my interest, but as I have gotten to know Thomas I have discovered he's actually a good guy. However, after tonight, I can't deny my feelings for Jason. Being with Jason and kissing him tonight felt familiar, it felt right. His warm touch and his soft lips on mine made me feel safe. What have I done? "Come on" Haley says bringing me back to reality as she loops her arm around mine, "you can't avoid mom and dad forever." "Ugh" I groan.

We approach another guest room that is four doors down from my room. Haley knocks and as we wait for them to open the door I can feel my palms start to sweat. "Sarah" my mother says as she opens the door. "Hello mom" I reply as she steps to the side and invites us in. Dad emerges from the closet and gives me a smile. "Hi sweetheart " he says while extending his arms out for a hug. I walk over and hug him which prompts a kiss to the top my head. "How are you?" He asks. "I'm good. When did you guys get in?" "About 30 minutes ago" he says. "Oh." "Where were you" my mother asks. "At a small carnival." "With Thomas?" she questions. "No mom, with a friend." "Ah, I see" she replies. "So how long are you guys down?" I ask. "Wow, ready for us to leave already" mother asks sharply. "Monday" Haley quickly adds, trying to break the tension. "Well, I'm sure you guys are tired, so I will let you get some rest. Goodnight." "Goodnight" they almost reply in unison. This is going to be the longest four days ever, I think to myself. I make my escape to my room and plop down on my bed and just stare at the ceiling. I think about everything that happened today. I should've just told Jason when it first happened, even if it was over phone. If I would have, there's a strong chance we would at least still be friends right now. Too late now. After an hour of wallowing in my own self-pity I get up and get things ready for tomorrow. On the bright side, I close at work tomorrow which means I won't be subjected to the family awkwardness for an extensive amount of time. I feel my phone buzz and quickly pull it out of my pocket. It's Thomas, but a small part of me was hoping it was Jason.

"Hi Thomas" "Hey Sarah, it's good to hear your voice." "Same here, how was practice?" "It was good, I think coach isn't playing around this year. He had us hit it hard today and already has a scrimmage planned for us this weekend." "Wow, that's intense. Too bad I have practice otherwise I'd come watch." "Ah, it's just a scrimmage. How was the carnival with Jason?" I could feel knots form in my stomach. "Um, it was fun. We had a good time, until we ran into Jess that is." "I'm sorry. What did she say?" "Oh, just how me and you are dating now and that I shouldn't be on dates with other guys." "Well that's hypocritical of her to say. Besides, I know Jason is your best friend. As jealous as it makes me at times, I would never keep you from hanging out with him." "That's sweet of you Thomas." There's a pause of silence between us. "I mean, you would tell me if anything were to happen between you two. Or anyone for that matter, right Sarah?" The image of me and Jason kissing on the Ferris Wheel pops in my head. "Of course, I would Thomas." I lie and I feel terrible. "Thank you, Sarah. And it's only fair that I be honest with you in return." "What do you mean?" I ask. "Remember when you asked me why I broke up with Jess?" "Yeah.." "Well, what I said was true, don't doubt it for a second. But, I had also found out Jess was seeing another guy behind my back. Granted, me and her did not have anything near the connection I feel with you, but it still hurt. When I confronted her about it, she said it was pay back for dumping her best friend and being careless with other girls' feelings. After that happened I realized how awful I had been and told myself I wanted to become a better me and start fresh." "Oh." I mean, I am essentially doing the same thing that Jess did to Thomas, not as a form of revenge but still. After tonight though, I can't say it's going to be much of a continuing occurrence. Maybe, it's a good thing me and Jason parted our ways. Now me and Thomas can focus on our relationship. "I hope you're not mad I didn't tell you the whole truth in the beginning. I was just ashamed and embarrassed." "No Thomas, I'm not mad. I'm glad that you told me though." "You are truly amazing Sarah. Thank you for understanding. Sorry, I didn't mean to drag this conversation on so long, I know you have an early day tomorrow." "That's okay, goodnight Thomas." "Goodnight, beautiful."

Chapter 8

The next day I try to go about my day as usual but knowing Jason is just a few classrooms down the hall made it hard to focus. "Miss Caldwell, are you having trouble inputting the data into the spreadsheet?" "Um, no Professor Mayhew. Sorry, I am just a bit distracted today is all." "I see that. Anything you want to talk about? I have some time after class." "I appreciate the offer sir, but this is something I'll have to figure out on my own. Thanks for bringing me back to reality though." I reply and start plugging in my data. He watches me for a moment and gives an approving nod before walking off. After class, I stand outside the door in hopes of running into Jason. A few minutes pass I finally see Jason emerge from class. He is heading in my direction until he notices me standing along the wall. He pauses for a moment and I give him a half smile with a small wave. He puts his headphones in and turns to walk in the opposite direction. Who am I kidding? I wouldn't forgive myself that easily either. I text Thomas to see if he wants to meet for lunch and he agrees.

"Hey you" Thomas says as takes a seat next to me. "Hey yourself." "This is a pleasant surprise. I thought you and Jason usually do lunch together?" "Um, well, he had to go take care of something." Wow, smooth lie Sarah. "Oh. Well, I'm not gonna complain about getting extra time with my girl" he says as he puts his hand on my thigh and as a reaction, my ears instantly get hot. I haven't been touched that intimately in what feels like forever. "What time do you think you'll get off tonight?" Thomas asks. "I'm not sure. Stacy says the carnival has slowed down business, so the owner may or may not have me close early tonight. But worst-case scenario 9:30. Why?" "Well I was thinking maybe we could go catch a movie afterwards, if you'd like?" As intriguing as that sounds, I knew I couldn't entirely avoid my family otherwise they would give a bad report to Dr. Loucheski. I also knew I couldn't let Thomas know they were in town because he would want to meet them. "I would love to Thomas, but I have some homework I need to work on since I have practice this weekend. Maybe we could do something Friday since I only work half the day?" "Sure babe, whatever works for you. But hey I gotta get going, I need to go print some stuff off at the library." He rises from the table and bends down to give me a kiss. As I turn back to my plate I notice Jason at the entrance of the cafeteria where he just shakes his head and walks off. Great, talk about perfect timing. I quickly get up and throw away my stuff, hoping that I might be able to catch up to Jason.

"Jason wait, please" I say as I catch up to him. He stops and turns around, "What Sarah?" "I… just, I don't know. I'm sorry is all. I didn't mean for any of this to happen." "For what to happen Sarah? For you to fall for some guy that looks like your dead ex or do you mean for you to string me along like a puppet?" "Any of it Jason. You were my first friend here and I opened up to you and I thought you respected that. I was and still am, in a vulnerable spot with my emotions. That's why it was so easy for my head to convince me to pursue Thomas. It doesn't help that he turned out to be a pretty good guy." "Well, that's really great Sarah. I hope the two of you live happily ever after then." "Stop it, Jason. I'm not finished, what I'm trying to say is I like you Jason. This whole time I had been slowly falling for you and I didn't realize it. After last night though it's hard for me to deny my feelings for you." We both stand there silently, looking at each other. "So, break it off with him. He's done it to plenty of girls, it's time he gets a taste of his own medicine anyway. Then, we can focus on us" he says. I let out a sigh. "It's not that easy Jason." "Why not?" "Because, he told me how he regrets his past and that he's trying to be a better person now. That I am his fresh start." "You have got to be kidding me. That is a load of crap. He's playing you Sarah." "No, he's not. After all, we are a couple. None of the other girls were his girlfriend, were they?" "No, they weren't." Jason replies through clenched teeth. "I just don't know what to do. I don't want to hurt his feelings, he's already opened up to me and taken me to meet his family." "I think you're asking the wrong person for advice, but what I can tell you is, you can't have both of us Sarah. I won't rush you, but, you are gonna have to make a decision eventually." "I know. I just don't want things to change between us in the meantime." "Well, you are in a relationship. It's not going to be easy, but I'll try to respect that. Are you sure you don't need space so you can make a clear decision?" "No!

Please, I would prefer it if we could maintain our friendship in the process." "Alright, just know I'm not going to make this easy on you," he says, giving me a mischievous smile, "I really need to get to class though so I'll talk to you later." I flash him a big smile, "okay great" I say.

After my last class, I make my way to work. So far, the only customers have been a handful of high school students stopping by after school let out but that's it. Stacy wasn't kidding, the carnival really has slowed down business. Better than being at home though. I make myself busy by organizing the freezers according to flavor and wiping down the machines. As I'm finishing up, I hear the door chime so I make my way back to the front. "Hi, welcome to froz...Haley what are you doing here?" "I thought I'd just stop by and see my favorite sister at work." "How did you know where I work?" "Hector told me." "Ah. I'm surprised mom and dad didn't wanna tag along." "I just told them I was going to the beach." We both let out a laugh. "Thanks for sparing me then." "So, what should I try?" I raise an eyebrow in response to her question. "What? You think I'm going to come all the way to your job just to say

hi?" I laugh "No I guess not. Um, I'd say the chocolate mixed with a little bit of the coconut is pretty good." "Mmm. That sounds delightful. I'll

take that please." It's a self-serve machine but I don't say anything as I

make it for her. She pays for it and takes a seat at one of the three tables

we have inside. "How was school?" She asks as she takes a big bite.

"Not too bad, it's good to be back, especially since I'm already so close

to being done." "I bet. And soccer?" "Well, we haven't started yet. Our

first practice is tomorrow." "Ooh, maybe I'll come watch." Haley teases.

"How are things back at home?" "Uh, boring. Definitely less drama now

that you're not there," she gives a small laugh, "I miss you though, that's

for sure." "I miss you too" I reply as I give her a warm smile. "As much

as I hated the thought of it, I'm glad to see that the move has really

helped you. I'm proud of you sis." "Thanks Haley." An awkward silence

falls between us. "Welp," she says rising from her chair "I think it's

time I let you get back to work." I glance at the vacant lobby. "Oh hush,

I wanna take a quick peek in some of these stores before I head back.

You know mom will get suspicious if I'm not back within a certain

time." I roll my eyes. "True. Thanks for stopping by though." I give her a hug which was long overdue because neither one of us pulled away for a couple seconds. "See ya tonight" she says as vanishes out the door.

Haley's visit was a pleasant surprise and it helped pass some time. I had one more customer after Haley and then around 6:30, Beth, the owner shows up. She reviews the customer count from yesterday and asks how many customers that I have had today and then decides we should close up early. She takes the till and tells me once I clean and lock up that I can go home. After I close up, I decide to stop by the surf shop to see if Jason is working.

When I enter the shop, I see Jason carrying a stack of boxes. "Would you like a hand?" The question startles him as he almost drops the boxes. "Geez Sarah. You scared the hell out of me." "Sorry, it looked like you were struggling." "Pfft. Me? Struggling? No way these are light as a feather." The sweat on his forehead said otherwise but I let him flaunt his masculinity as reassurance. "What are you doing here?" he asks as he places the boxes next to some other ones. "The boss let me close early, so I figured I'd stop by on my way out." "Nice. I would be jealous but I'm honestly glad to finally be getting some hours." "That's good." "Sure is. So, what are you gonna do with all your free time?" "I guess head home. Even though that's the last place I wanna be." "Woah, is everything okay?" "It's just my parents and sister are in town and it's more of a welfare check than an 'I miss you and just wanted to see you' type of check." "I'm sorry Sarah, I'm sure I didn't make the situation any better either." "It's okay, you didn't know." He grabs my hand, "everything is going to be okay. How long are they down?" "Till Monday." "Sheesh, two more days after today. You can do it though." "I hope so. It just seems so far away." "Anything I can do to help?" Jason asks. "I guess just listen to me complain, per usual." "I think I can manage that" he replies as he takes a step closer to me while gazing into my eyes. I wanted nothing more than for him to kiss me right then but instead he gives my hand a little squeeze and then backs away. I'd be lying if I said I wasn't disappointed, but it was for the better. Kissing Jason had awoken a burning passion inside me that hasn't been fulfilled since before Jake's passing and now I couldn't help but crave more. The only problem is, will I be able to control myself around Thomas for the time being? "Well I guess I better get going." "That's probably a good idea." Jason says, giving me a smirk.

I make it home close to eight and head straight to the kitchen to make a quick meal for dinner. "Oh, there she is!" Grandma exclaims, "doesn't she look cute as a button in her uniform?" "Of course, she does" dad replies. "Hi grandma, hi dad." "How was your day sweet pea?" Dad asks. "Not too shabby I guess." "That's good to hear." The kitchen falls silent and I could tell he was hesitating for a reason. "Everything okay dad?" "Well I know you're not necessarily ecstatic that we are here, but I was hoping we would be able to spend some time together before we leave?" "Dad I wouldn't mind, but, I had no idea you guys were coming so my schedule is kind of tight. Tomorrow I have work and soccer practice." I could see the look of sadness spread across his face and I felt bad. This wasn't his fault, if anything, he was the one trying to reach out to me and I was being an ass. "But Sunday I think I'm pretty much free." There was a noticeable perk in his demeanor. "Are you sure? I would hate to mess up your plans." "I'm positive dad."

I say as I give him a kiss on the cheek and tell him goodnight before heading upstairs.

Chapter 9

The next day I get off work at two and instead of going to the movies me and Thomas decide to hang out at his parent's house until I have to leave for practice. Once I arrive, I quickly regret my decision when I find out his parents aren't home. At first, we talk about soccer, then my work, and afterwards we share stories about our childhood. I shouldn't be entertaining the thought of prolonging this relationship with Thomas, but I feel so bad. His honesty and sweet demeanor hasn't helped this decision. Our conversation dies down when a movie that intrigues us comes on. We then find ourselves cuddling on the sofa. Half way through I feel Thomas start to caress my arm. I try to ignore it by focusing intensely on the screen but then he kisses me on my neck, triggering goosebumps all over my body. I give in and look into his eyes and he pulls me onto his lap as he starts to kiss me intensely. You can't do this, I think to myself. This will only make it harder to break things off. His lips start to make their way down to my chest but just as he tries to pull my shirt up, I stop him.

"I'm sorry Thomas, I don't think I'm ready yet." He rubs the back of his neck, "Gee, I'm sorry Sarah, I hope I didn't make you uncomfortable." "No, not at all. Things are just moving a little fast is all." "Well we can totally slow things down. I wouldn't want to ruin anything because of my own selfish desires." I blush, "thanks for understanding Thomas" I say as I give him a kiss on the cheek. It feels good to know I am wanted but I can't let my emotions, or sexual urges for that matter, get in the way of making a sound decision. "I better get going though, I don't want to chance being late for the first practice." "Oh right, can I walk you out?" "Of course." He picks up my bag and carries it for me as we make our way to the car. "Let me know how it goes" he says, then giving me a kiss on the forehead. "I will. Have fun at your scrimmage tonight." "Yes ma'am." He gives me a smile and shuts my door once I'm in.

Practice was fun and it was nice getting back on the field. I could tell I was still pretty out of shape because by time we were done, it felt like my lungs were on fire. I was grateful Jess didn't make the team because that means I don't have to put up with her devious, snarky remarks. It just doesn't add up though. If she was doing it as revenge, why is she so bitter about me being with Thomas? Oh well. I start to pack up my bag and decide I'll just shower at home.

"Hey Sarah!" "Oh, hey Stacy!" "You were awesome out there." "Aw, thanks girl. I see they let you be assistant team manager." "Yeah, it's been pretty cool so far." "That's great, glad to have you as part of the team!" "Thanks!" She replies with a big smile and then it slowly fades as her gaze falls to the ground and she starts to pick at her nails. "So, um, I don't mean to be weird but do you think Jason would be interested in going on date with me?" I stop what I'm doing and let out a chuckle, "Um what do you mean?" "Well I just know you two are pretty close and I wasn't sure if he was seeing or dating anyone, so I thought I'd ask you." Damn it Stacy, why are you doing this to me? She is such a sweet girl and it's not fair of me to interfere, but it kills me inside to give her the green-light to pursue Jason. "Oh, right. Well all he's told me is he's interested in someone, but he hasn't mentioned any names." There that's a pretty neutral answer. "Oh okay cool, well I guess that means I still have a shot" she says as she lets out a little giggle. I just laugh in return.

"Well, I'm pretty beat but I'll catch you around Stacy." "Alright, later girl!" Is it wrong of me to be jealous? After all, I'm in a relationship with another guy.

Once I make it home I head straight for the shower. I take off all my clothes and stare at my reflection in the mirror. I grab the chain around my neck and slowly take it off and for the first time in 10 months, I feel entirely exposed. I look at the ring laying in the palm of my hand and it triggers so many emotions. I close my hand tightly around the ring and bring it up to my mouth, pressing my lips to my clenched hand as I start to cry. I lay the necklace carefully on the counter and turn the shower on. I step in and let the water fall upon my numb body. What people didn't realize, or should I say, what I chose not to tell people, is that Jake had planned on proposing to me the night of the accident. I remember it all too well.

At first, I think I blacked out since I had been drinking, but when I come thru I feel a wetness dripping down my face. I touch my forehead and when I pull my hand away, there's blood. I look over at Jake in the driver's seat. "Jake" I manage to say but he doesn't move. "Jake!" I

shout while nudging his shoulder. He groans as he starts to wake up.
"What happened?" "I think we were in an accident Jake. We need to
call for help." We both start feeling for our phones. "Found mine" I say
as I dial 911. "Hi uh me and my boyfriend were just in a car accident
and we are bleeding pretty bad. No, I'm not sure where we are at, it's
dark and we are surrounded by trees." I turn to Jake, "do you know
where we are?" "I think we should be pretty close to Versailles." I relay
the information to the operator. My phone beeps and displays a low bat-
tery warning. "Ma'am you have to hurry my phone is on five percent."
The operator proceeds to repeat 'stay calm, we have multiple units out
searching for you' and keeps asking me questions to keep me alert and
calm until my phone dies. "Damnit." I say throwing my phone to the
floorboard. "It's okay Sarah, they are going to find us." "Jake your
head is bleeding badly and your shoulder looks distorted, this isn't
good." "Are you okay though?" he asks me. "My forehead is bleeding a
little and my right-side hurts pretty bad but I think that's it" I tell
him. "You know I love you right?" He tells me. "Jesus Jake. Don't start
talking like that." He laughs and then immediately grimaces as he

clenches his stomach. *"I'm not, I just wanted to make sure you know."*
"I do, and I love you too" I say as I start to cry. "Come on babe don't
cry, it's gonna be okay." "I know, I'm just scared and upset. Why were
we even going towards Versailles in the first place?" I say angrily.
"Well" he pauses for a moment, "I hope you give me a chance for a do-
over." "What are you talking about?" I ask as Jake starts digging in his
pocket and pulls out a small box. "I know how much you love that castle
they have there, and I thought it would be the perfect place to ask you to
be my princess forever." He says as he opens the box and reveals a shiny
ring that I knew cost way more than he could afford. Now I really let the
tears fall. "Jake are you serious?" He hands me the box, "I've never
been more serious. Now what do you say?" I nod excessively and give
him a huge smile as he slides the ring on my finger but it quickly fades
as I notice head lights approaching us and the sound of a horn start to
blare. "Jake" I scream, but it didn't matter, it is too late. Another car T-
bones us on Jake's side of the car.

Unbeknown to us, the first car that rear ended us, hit us so hard it
pushed us into the middle of an intersection. They of course fled the

scene and didn't alert anyone. Which in turn, put us in the perfect spot to get hit by the second car, who happened to be flying through the intersection because 'usually no one is out there after dark.' Even though I've turned the bathroom into a sauna, I still shutter as the memory crosses my mind. I turn the water off, get dressed, grab my belongings, and head to my room.

I told myself I would never take this chain off, yet here I am tucking it safely away in my night stand. With the way things are between Thomas and Jason, I figured it's not appropriate for me to be clinging on to the past. This is my next step of moving forward and despite the strong feelings I feel for the each of them, it still hurt so damn bad. I sit down and try to work on some homework to get my mind off it all. After about an hour, I get a text from Thomas.

Hey babe, just got home. Scrimmage went good, we won 3-2. How was practice?

That's good. It went fine, I definitely need to start running though.

Lol same here. So, what are you up to?

Just working on some homework. You?

Well I was going to see if you wanted to talk but I don't want to distract you. I may just shower and hit the hay.

Ok, goodnight. I'll talk to you tomorrow.

Goodnight beautiful.

Once I finish my homework I lay down and start to browse social media. I come across a post scrimmage selfie of Thomas and I can't help but think to myself how attractive he is. Simultaneously, this triggers the desire to look at photos of Jason and that's when I realize I am not friends with Jason on social media. I try to look him up, but I can't find him on anything. Hmm, that's odd. Oh well, I decide to call it a night and get some sleep.

The next morning, I take my time getting ready. I wonder what dad could possibly have planned for the family to do today but whatever it is, I hope it goes smoothly. I make a pledge to myself to put my best foot forward today, but of course that could all go out the window depending on how mom behaves. I take one deep breath and make my way down to the kitchen. As I round the corner I see Haley and our grandparents already eating breakfast. "Good morning Sarah" grandpa says. "Good morning" I reply. "Oh, Sarah those arrived for you just a little bit ago" grandma adds while nodding past me. I turn around and see a beautiful arrangement of sunflowers and red roses mixed together. I walk over and read the card attached.

Sorry for yesterday. May today be as beautiful as you are. -Thomas

I feel myself smiling. That was sweet of him. "Are those from Thoooomas?" I hear Haley ask. I turn around and can feel myself blushing. "Yes, they are" I say. "He seems like a keeper." Haley replies. "Who's a keeper?" Dad says as him and mom emerge into the kitchen. "Sarah's boyfriend. He sent her those flowers." "My those are beautiful" mother comments. "Well I sure would like to meet him, you can invite him out with us today. I was thinking maybe catch a movie, grab an early dinner, and explore the pier. It's been forever since I've been down there." "That sounds great dad, but unfortunately Thomas won't be able to make it. Today is their first away game." I lied, but all I knew was that I had to keep them from meeting. "Oh, well dang. Today is supposed to be a family day anyway." I start to wonder though, maybe this is a sign that I shouldn't be with Thomas. If I have to go through this much trouble because I'm afraid of what my family will think, then how can we realistically be together in the long-term sense of things. Is that a valid reason to break up with someone though, especially when it's not even their fault? I glance over at the flowers and feel a wave of guilt overcome me. This is going to be a tough decision.

As we go about our day, Haley clings to me trying to keep me occupied so that me and mom don't butt heads. Luckily, there's no talking during a movie which means there's an even less chance of us getting in an argument. I'm sure that was clever planning on dad's behalf. After the movies we agree on a seafood restaurant close to the pier that google deemed a popular favorite. Mother remains unusually quiet throughout the dinner, only commenting on the food and what she would like to see and do when we go to the pier. Not sure if she was behaving herself due to an audience being present or if she finally realizes how exhausting it is to fight. Either way, so far, today has been decent. Once we make it to the pier we treat ourselves to some tasty junk food as dessert and make our way down the boardwalk. Dad and Haley end up wanting to ride the rollercoaster and giant Ferris Wheel. I thought I was afraid on the smaller one with Jason, I couldn't imagine riding the one on the pier. This is where me and mom actually share a common interest because neither one of us likes heights. Dad and Haley go off to fulfill their adrenaline junkie needs while me and mom are left standing awkwardly in the middle of the pier. We decide to go browse some shops to pass the time.

"So, how are you liking it here?" mom asks. "I don't mind it. It's different though." "I can imagine. It's not like Kentucky at all." "No, not even close." A moment of silence passes between us before she speaks again. "It seems like you are settling in nicely though. You have a new school, new job, new boyfriend. Looks like a fresh start is exactly what you needed Sarah." Oh yeah, because she knows exactly what I needed. After the accident she didn't even want to look at me. She called me a murderer and a reckless alcoholic and thought I needed to be sent away for good. She was more preoccupied trying to restore our family's name, as if rejecting me would somehow right the wrong I did. I hold my tongue though and give a her a fake smile, "I guess so mom." Fortunately, by time we finish browsing our third shop, dad calls to tell us they are finished and where to meet them. Once we are all together again we agree to head back up the pier.

"So, where's the shop you work at Sarah?" mom asks. "Um, a little ways up just off the main strip." "Mind if we stop and take a peek?" Dad interjects. "There's not much to it but sure." At least this way they can meet Stacy and have that sense of involvement in my new life that they are craving so badly. When we approach the shop, it is empty and I can see Stacy sweeping the floor.

"Hi welcome to Frozen Swirl...oh hey Sarah!" "Hey Stacy, I'd like to introduce you to my parents and my sister Haley." "Well hello every-one, nice to meet you" Stacy says. "Pleasure to meet you Stacy" mom replies. "I'm actually glad you popped in Sarah, can I show you some-thing in the back." "Sure thing." "Sorry Mr. and Mrs. Caldwell it won't take long." "You're fine sweetie" dad says. Once we make it to the back storeroom, Stacy turns to me frantically. "I need your advice!" "What's wrong?" I ask. "Sooo, I texted Jason asking if he could come over once he gets off." "Okay..." "I planned on asking him if he wants to go on a date." "Ah I see." I say as I could feel my heart sink a little. "But, I don't know how to ask him. I don't want to come off as too forward, but, I still want to get across to him that I'm interested." "Maybe just tell him that you'd like to get to know him better and was wondering if you two could hang out or something." "Oh, that is perfect, thanks so much Sarah!" She exclaims as she embraces me in a hug. I hug her and tell her I should probably get back to my family. "You guys ready?" I ask as we emerge from the back, but my question is unheard as my family is pre-occupied talking. I guess we didn't hear the door chime because Jason is there in the lobby conversing with my parents.

"Oh, hey Sarah, hey Stacy." "Hey Jason" we say unison. "Jason was just telling us that you were his first friend here." "She was techni-cally mine too!" Stacy adds. "See, she's been nothing but a blessing, I don't know what I would do without her" Jason says. I can't help but blush. "Awe, thanks you two. I am sure glad it was their idea to stop by otherwise they'd think I paid you two." The entire room erupts with laughter. "We better get going though so Stacy can get back to work." I

say, trying to escape from anymore small talk. "See ya around." Stacy
says as Jason gives me a small wave and his charming smile.

"Well they seem like nice people." Dad says. "And that Jason boy
seems to fancy you." Mom adds, "Yeah, we are pretty close. He's been a
good friend to me." I say. "Mhm." Is all mom says before I change the
subject. "Thanks for today dad, it was a lot of fun." "Well you're welcome sweet pea." "Yeah thanks dad" Haley adds. We finally make it to
the car and start our journey home. During the ride home I get a text
from Jason.

Stacy just asked me out

I know…who do you think she asked for advice?

Ouch. So, you helped her ask me out?

*Yeah talk about salt in the wound, but it would've been selfish of me not
to.*

Wow, I think I grow more attracted to you each day.

What did you tell her?

I said yes…but I swear she like inner channeled some puppy dog eyes and I felt too bad to say no.

See it's not as easy as you think it is to reject someone.

Touche, but I'm gonna let her know that I'm only interested as a friend.

Just be nice, she really likes you.

"Who's that?" Haley asks. "Just Jason." She gives me a devious side eye. "What?" I ask. "I saw the way you two looked at each other. There's more than friendship between y'all and I know it." "I'm dating Thomas." I scoff, feeling slightly offended, but also flattered. "He sure is cute though, I can only imagine what Thomas looks like." "Geez Haley, I'm not that superficial." "Sorry, that's not what I was getting at." She says as turns to stare out her window. I let out a sigh. "I know you better than you think. So why don't you tell me what's wrong?" She pauses for a moment as if she is contemplating if she should tell me. "Me and Evan broke up." "What? When? Why?" "A week before we decided to come here. I found out he was cheating so I told him we were done, and I never wanted to see him again." She says matter-of-factly. "I am so sorry Haley." "It's okay, it's not your fault he was a sleaze bag." Haley and Evan were high school sweethearts and had been together for eight years. We always wondered why Evan wouldn't propose but I guess we found out why. "I know, but I should've been there to comfort you." "I'm okay. Really, it's kind of a relief honestly. That's why I was so eager to come out here and see if I could find me an LA cutie." We both laugh.

Chapter 10

It's finally Monday and despite the visit going relatively well, I am relieved they are heading back home. It was just a matter of time before the facade of one big happy family wore off and true colors were shown. I wish Haley could have stayed though. I tried to talk her into it since it seems like she could use a fresh start of her own, but, she just laughed and told me not to worry. After they leave, I try to decide what to do since there is no class today. Not long after, I get a text from Jason asking if he could come over. Jason has been over multiple times, but, this would be the first time he would be over since we shared our feelings for one another and the thought of it made my heart race a little.

Just as I finish getting ready the doorbell rings, so I make my way down. "Hey" I say as I open the door. "Hey" Jason says giving me a big smile. "Oh, uh, come in." I say stepping to the side to let him through. "So, to what do I owe the pleasure?" I ask as we make our way into the kitchen. "I just really wanted to see you." I give him a warm smile. "Well I wanted to see you too. I've just been preoccupied with my family." "I know. I'm glad I got a chance to meet them though, especially since I have to compare up to Thomas." "Actually...they didn't meet Thomas. I didn't want them to." "Really? Why?" "Because he looks too much like Jake and I was afraid they would assume I'm only with him because of it." "Well... aren't you?" "Maybe at first, but like I already told you, he's actually a pretty good guy once you get to know him." I could feel myself getting defensive. I hate that everyone is making me out to be some superficial shallow person. "Yeah apparently so." He says nodding towards the arrangement of flowers. "They're just apology flowers Jason." "For what? Not being Mr. Nice guy after all?" "No! They were for...something else." This was such an uncomfortable conversation. He cocked his head at me indicating he was waiting for a response. "I…he…we just had a hot and heavy moment and I stopped it before anything really happened and I told him that things were moving too fast. I guess he felt really bad, so he sent me flowers to apologize." Jason just stood there and let out a large huff. "Well alrighty then. I guess I didn't realize you two were on that level already." "We're not. I just told you I stopped it. Geez what's your deal?" "I'm sorry. I didn't come here to argue. It just kills me Sarah. You don't think I wouldn't love to be in Thomas' shoes? It's painful to watch him touch you, hug you, kiss you, hell just the mere fact he gets to call you his hurts." I could see the frustration burrow in his brows. I couldn't think of the right words to say so I hugged him. He tries to back away, but I only hug him tighter, not wanting to let go. He cradles my head between his hands and raises my head so that our eyes meet. Any will power I have, disappears in that instance as I kiss Jason. At first, he kisses me back softly but as the moment of passion brews, our kisses turn sloppy. He picks me up and sits me on the counter as he starts to kiss along my neck. I wrap my legs around his waist pulling him closer to me. Suddenly, the doorbell rings, startling us both. Jason helps me off the counter and clears his throat. "Are you gonna get that?" "Um yeah" I say as I straighten my shirt and run my fingers through my hair.

Mesmerized by what just happened I make my way to the door. I can't believe we just did that, in the middle of the kitchen of all places. It's like all my inhibitions go out the window when I'm with Jason and it can't help but remind me of how risqué Jake and I were. I mean how far would things have gone if the doorbell didn't interrupt us? As I open the door, Thomas is standing on the porch. "Um, Thomas, hi. What are you doing here?" "Sorry, I know this is unexpected, but I just wanted to surprise you. I feel like I haven't seen you all weekend and I just wanted to make sure everything was good between us?" "Oh, yeah, everything is fine. I just picked up an extra shift at work." "Oh, whew, okay good. Mind if I come in?" "Oh, yeah, of course" I give a slight laugh. "Jason just got here not too long ago, if you want to join us in the kitchen."

"Hey dude." Thomas says as he precedes to give Jason a typical 'bro' shake. "What's up man?" "Oh ya know just thought I'd drop by and see this beauty." Thomas says as he puts his arm around me. "So, what are y'all up to on this fine day? Hopefully I didn't interrupt up anything" I give a nervous laugh while Jason shakes his head. "I just thought I'd stop by and get Sarah's advice for my date tonight." "My man, look at you goin on a date. Who with?" "Stacy. Sarah's co-worker." "Right on. Good luck man." "Thanks." Thomas takes a step forward and turns around to face me. "Ah good you got the flowers! I was worried maybe they didn't make it." With Thomas' back to Jason, Jason gives an eye-roll. I want to laugh but I channel it into a smile. "Yeah! They're beautiful. Thank you, I meant to text you, but it's been a crazy weekend." "That's okay babe he says as he gives me a kiss. My eyes quickly dart to Jason as I see him pretend to vomit. "Well once you're finished helping Jason, how about we go on a date ourselves?" "Uh, sure, that would be nice." "Great! Well, I just wanted to check on you, but I guess I'll let y'all get down to it then." "Oh yeah, time to get down and dirty Sarah" Jason says. Thomas lets out a little chuckle. "Have fun tonight Jason." "Here, let me walk you out babe." I say as I loop my arm around Thomas' and lead him to the door. "Do you mind meeting me at my place and then I can drive us?" Thomas asks. "That's not a problem, I'll see you tonight" I say. "I can't wait" he says as he gives me another kiss. "Me either, see you later." I watch him get in his car and give a wave before shutting the door.

Jason emerges from around the corner. I cross my arms and shake my head. "What?" He asks. "Down and dirty. Really? You just had to say that?" He laughs, "it was a play on words." I roll my eyes. "You should feel terrible. You're about to go on a date." "And you have a boyfriend" he replies. "I know. Way to make me feel like the worst girl-friend in the world." "You wouldn't have to feel that way if you would quit fooling yourself and break up with him already." "Come on, look how happy he is. It's not that easy." "Well yeah, I'd be that happy too if you were my girlfriend." Ugh. He sure knows how flatter a person. "Will you stop that?" I ask. "Stop what? Being honest?" "You're not making this easy. I need time. After all I'm in the middle of breaking someone's heart." "Hey, I told you this wasn't going to be easy." "I know, and I appreciate you being so patient" I say. "I already waited my whole life, what's a little bit longer" he replies. I blush and look at the floor, trying to avoid looking him in the eyes. "Please be nice to Stacy and take this date seriously, she is a good person." "You know I will. I just plan on letting her know that what me and her share is more of a friendship and that I am interested in somebody else." "You never know Jason, you could really enjoy your time with her and want to pursue a relationship with her." "You're right." I give him a bewildered look. "What? So, you're the only one who can pursue two people at once? After all it might make you realize what you're missing." Jason says as he gives his arms a slight flex. I roll my eyes, "oh yeah because you're all that and a bag of chips huh?" He gives me his heart melting smile, "well I haven't heard any complaints from you so far" he replies as he gives me a wink. I give him a smirk and turn to walk off when he grabs me by the hand. "Wait where are you going?" "Um to my room." "Is that an invitation?" He asks giving me a mischievous grin. "Only if you behave" I tell him. Jason lets out a sigh, "if you say so." When we make it to my room Jason starts making his way around looking at all of my things. Even though Jason has been over multiple times, he's never been in my room and now that we've obliterated the boundary of being 'just friends' having him in my bedroom made me nervous. I see him open my journal that I have laying on my desk and I rush over and snatch it from him.

"That's off limits." "Sorry. I can't help but want to know more of you. I want to know your deep thoughts, your dreams, everything. I just can't get enough of you Sarah." "Well maybe if you'd start opening up to me Jason, then I'd do the same." "What is that supposed to mean?" "Don't act like you don't have any secrets yourself. You have sketchy phone calls and you get all weird and upset when I bring up certain things about your personal life. I feel like I don't even know you sometimes." "Please don't say that Sarah. I don't want to keep things from you, but there's things that have to do with my life that I can't tell anyone. It's out of my hands." "What does that even mean? You're telling me that even if we were dating you'd still keep secrets from me?" "It wouldn't be by choice. It's for my own safety and yours. Surely you wouldn't want me to risk my safety or even possibly yours just so that way there are no secrets between us." "Of course not, but, I can't help but worry about you. How do I know if you're not involved in some kind of serious trouble. Like, are you a criminal running from the law, are you drug dealer? I just hate not knowing." He starts to chuckle, "I promise you, it's nothing like that. It's just if I'm not careful, my past mistakes could catch up with me." I remain silent so he pulls me into a hug and kisses my forehead. "I wish I could tell you, but I wouldn't forgive myself if anything happened to you." "I understand" I say as I try to pull away, but now it's Jason that won't let go. As I look up, I meet his blue eyes that are staring down at me. I wanted nothing more than to kiss him, but now that we were alone in the privacy of my room who knows how far things would go or if I'd be willing to stop myself. He kisses me softly, sending jolts of electricity throughout my entire body which triggers me to kiss him back. I press myself against his muscular body and I run my fingers through his luscious dirty blonde shaggy hair. In that instance I couldn't feel any more comfortable. He kisses along my neck and works his way up to nibble on my ear. I let out a small groan. "Jason, not now, this isn't right." My eyes were still closed, but I could feel him let out a sigh. "As you wish," he says as he takes a step back and kisses my hand. "I guess I better get going, so we can get ready for our 'dates,'" Jason says using air quotes. "Okay" I reply, while staring at the ground to avoid the sweet seduction of his blue eyes. I don't want him to leave, but it's for the better.

As the adrenaline rush starts to wear off, the guilt settles in. What kind of terrible person can cheat on their significant other like that and then turn around and pretend like nothing has happened. I'm no better than Evan, my sister's douche-bag of an ex. I am attracted to Thomas for a reason and I need to give him a fair shot before I make up my mind so easily. I shake my head trying to get rid of all my negative thoughts. I never imagined I would be in a situation like this. A year ago, I was madly in love with the man I swore I was going to spend the rest of my life with and now here I am stuck in some twisted love triangle with two guys I've only known for a few short months. What is wrong with me? I start to get ready now that it's approaching four 'o'clock and I want to avoid the LA traffic on the way to Thomas's. I finally settle on some faded denim capris and an off the shoulder blouse that makes me feel cute. I curl my hair and put on some mascara, nothing over the top but definitely putting more into my appearance than I have since my interviews when I first got here. I wasn't sure if it is my guilty subconscious that is motivating me, but I want to surprise Thomas by looking my best. I certainly haven't given him my best so I need to give this relationship my all, that way I can make a sound decision. Once I finish getting ready I grab my keys and make my way to Thomas's.

I pull up in the round about and make my way to the door. A few moments after I knock, Thomas's mom answers the door. "Hi Teresa" I say giving her I smile. "Well hey there sweetie" she says as she finishes applying here earrings and steps aside to welcome me in. "I think Thomas is almost finished getting ready. David is expecting some clients over here shortly, so you are welcome to wait in his room if you'd like." "Alrighty," I reply as I start to look around deciding which direction I should take first. Teresa lets out a light chuckle, "follow me sweetie I'll show you where it's at," once she realizes I have no idea where his room is. "Would you mind though?" She says pointing towards her back and turning to reveal her unzipped dress. "Oh sure," I say as I zip her up. As I do, I notice a tattoo along her shoulder that says 'Gone but never for-gotten' with a heart at the end. I assume it's in memory of Emily, and I can't help but feel my heart ache for this family. Which is another reason I felt bad for not giving Thomas a fair shot. He has already lost someone he cares about once already, how could I do it to him again? We make it to Thomas's room just as the door bell sends a melodic tune throughout the house once more. "Make yourself comfortable and enjoy your date," she says as she gives me a quick peck on the cheek and rushes back down stairs. I turn to look at Thomas's room. It was for the most part tidy with a few socks scattered here and there. His desk is cluttered with papers and books and his dresser is topped with numerous soccer trophies and a few baseball trophies from a couple years back. I see a photo of Thomas and his sister that sits on his night stand. It was a candid shot of him and her laughing and I could tell she was naturally beautiful, she looked so carefree and friendly.

"Sarah!" My thoughts are interrupted as I hear Thomas say my name, I spin around to see him standing in his door way in nothing but a towel. Oh my, I think to myself. I knew I should close my eyes or turn back around, but I can't take my eyes off him. His hair is still dripping wet and my eyes couldn't help but trail downward discovering his rock-hard abs and a perfectly sculpted v-line that had my imagination trying to fill the void of the only part of his body that isn't revealed. "I, uh, your mom told me I could wait here." I stammer. He gives me a smirk, which let me know I was caught. He knew I was checking him out. "Oh, I'm not complaining." He says as he ventures further into his room, making the distance between him and I less and less. As he gets closer, I have to shift my weight from side to side, trying to release the tension I felt growing below. "You look beautiful babe" he says as he approaches me and gives me a kiss on the lips. I could smell the scent of cleanliness, but he still possessed an aroma of masculinity. "Thanks, you, um, look good too" I say. "Hey my eyes are up here," he says jokingly while taking a step back. I can't help but laugh and his joke seems to ease some of the tension I was feeling. Lord, I hope he can't read my thoughts right now. "Sorry it's just been awhile since I've had a handsome practically naked man in my presence." "Don't be sorry, I'm glad you like what you see. I was starting to worry you weren't as attracted to me as I was to you." "Why would you say that?" I ask astonishingly. He grabs some boxers out of his dresser and goes in his closet to get dressed. "I don't know, it's just every time I have tried to show you affection I feel like it scares you off as if you aren't attracted to me in that way. Not that I would ever expect anything more than what you are comfortable with. I just wasn't sure if it was me or not." He finally emerges from the closet in some dark jeans and a t-shirt that molded perfectly to his lean yet muscular build. "Oh my gosh, no! It's not you at all, in fact you're almost so perfect it's scary. I'm just struggling internally with things." He gives me a frown. "I hate that you feel like you have to struggle alone. I am always here for you if I can help you in anyway." Oh yeah Thomas, please help me decide whether I should break your heart and run straight into Jason's arms or not, I think to myself. "Thank you, Thomas, but this is something I have to deal with on my own. I appreciate you being so patient and understanding." "Of course, beautiful." "Are you ready?" I ask as I put my hand out for him to grab. He takes my hand in his and pulls me close to him. "You mean am I ready to have the most beautiful girl I've ever seen all to myself tonight? You better believe it." He sure is a charmer and I feel bad for not giving this relationship my all because he sure is a sweet guy and his feelings towards me have been genuine. I put my arms around his neck and reply with a kiss. He slides his hands down to my waist and pulls my body to his as he kisses me back. Despite his warm kisses, I have goosebumps all over as he slides his hand up my shirt and traces my bra strap with his finger. Have I just been so deprived of affection since Jake's death that my hormones have me raging like a sexually frustrated teenager? Mid kiss Thomas lifts me from the ground and turns, sitting me on his bed. I grab Thomas by his waist band, pulling him onto the bed with me as I start to kiss his neck and run my hands up and down his back. Thomas then uses one hand to reach up the front of my shirt to fondle my breast. The tension I had previously felt was now back and it was only growing stronger and stronger. As I push my body against his I can feel that I am not the only one that is excited. Thomas's breath gets heavier on my neck as I tug on his waistband, hinting that I was eager for more. I feel Thomas come to a sudden stop and I open my eyes to see him hovering over me with a smile. "What?" I ask. "As much as I enjoy how well this is going, I don't want to take things too far and have you regret taking things too fast. The last thing I wanna do is scare you off." Why did he have to be so thoughtful? He was right though, I don't want to look back on a heated moment of lust and regret it. I want my next time being with someone to be meaningful and passionate not sloppy and thoughtless. "Thank you, Thomas"

I say, giving him one last kiss before he pulls himself off me. "Of course, Sarah. I want our first time to be special and not something that feels rushed" Thomas replies as he stands and turns his back to me. I can't help but blush at the realization that he has to adjust himself to hide the excitement of unfinished business. It makes me wonder if he was like this with the women he was previously with. Was he as thoughtful and sensitive as he was with me? And how many has he slept with? I shake my head to erase the thoughts from my mind. "Let's go" he says as he pulls me up from his bed.

Chapter 11

My date with Thomas was quite enjoyable. He had made us reservations at a romantic little restaurant and afterwards we went and saw the latest rom-com that was showing. After the movie we decided we didn't want the night to end, so, we made a pit stop for some ice cream which gave of us the opportunity to engage in long over-due, deep conversation. By the end of the night I couldn't help but feel more attracted to Thomas than I thought I would. He was chivalrous, opening every door we came across, and the compliments were endless up until I left his house. I was smiling like an idiot and even my grandparents noticed I was in an exceptionally good mood but knew not to pry and just simply stated, "we like this Sarah."

I was getting ready for bed when it dawned on me that Jason and Stacy went on a date too and I couldn't help but wonder how it went. There was part of me that wanted it to go well between the two of them, so I didn't have so much pressure on me to make this decision so quickly, but, at the same time I was jealous because I wanted Jason all to myself. I end up sending Jason a text.

How'd the date go?

I mean I didn't expect him to respond right away but after an hour passes and midnight approached, I figure I don't need to keep waiting. When I wake up the next morning there is still no text from Jason. Strange. I get up and get ready for class. Today's Tuesday so me and Jason don't have class together but we always meet at our designated bench and chat at before we have to head to class.

I take our usual seat and wait for Jason to show up. Ten minutes before class is supposed to start, I hear a familiar giggle come from across the way and when I look up I see Stacy and Jason standing next to the vending machines. Wait is she wearing his hoodie? I can't hear what they're saying, but I see her give him a quick kiss on his cheek before turning to leave. I quickly flip open my book to act like I have been reading. My mind starts to race. Had their date gone a little too well and extended into an overnight stay? That would explain why he hadn't texted back.

As Jason approaches the bench he clears his throat. "Hey you." "Hey yourself." I say as cheerily as I can. "Did I miss something we were supposed to read over?" He asks while looking down at my book. "Oh, uh, no. You know me, just reading ahead." "Nerd." He scoffs. I offer a forced half laugh, "well I better get going to to class or I'll be late, see you at lunch I guess?" I say. "Yeah, see you then" Jason says.

When class is over we meet up once again and make our way to the cafeteria per our usual routine for lunch. "Um, do you mind if Stacy joins us?" Jason asks as we make our way through the checkout line. "Not at all" I say while trying to convince myself I wasn't jealous. Isn't this what I wanted after all? We make our way to a table and it isn't long before Stacy joins us and to no surprise she takes a seat right next to Jason. They exchange smiles to one another before Jason finishes his rant over the lack of variety in condiments the school had to offer. After about ten minutes of awkwardly listening to Stacy conversate with Jason as if I wasn't in front of them, I feel a kiss on top of my head. When I look up I see Thomas standing over me. "Hey Thomas" I say. "I thought I'd come join you guys, so my babe didn't feel like such a third wheel." Stacy giggles and rubs up against Jason, being pleased with the idea that they were coming off as a couple. Whatever, Thomas was my boyfriend and she had Jason, so everything worked out. I put my hand on Thomas's thigh showing him I appreciate his presence. "Also, I wanted to invite you all over to my place tonight. My parents are letting me have a party tonight to celebrate the start of the season and it's gonna be pretty hype." Tonight, is both mine and Thomas' first game of the season and they're at home nonetheless. I can't believe I almost let it slip my mind. "Let's go to it!" Stacy pleads to Jason. Jason looks at me and I quickly direct my gaze to Thomas. "I'll be there babe. I mean I kinda have no excuse since ladies play first" I say. I see Jason simultaneously nod his head in response to Stacy's request. "Great!" Thomas exclaims and the smile on his face let me know he only cared that I would be there. We then discuss how ready we are for the game and how last year the opposing team went almost undefeated with the exception of one loss. I wonder how much playing time I'll get, being a newbie on the team on all. This will be my first debut in roughly three years, I hope I don't make a fool of myself.

I finally finish my last class of the day and head to the library to work on some assignments. As I'm passing through the courtyard I see Jason heading in the same direction, so I quicken my pace so I can catch up to him. I knew better than to call his name because he more than likely had his headphones in. When I reach him, I tap him on the shoulder and he spins to face me. "Oh, hey Sarah." "Hey" is all I can manage to say as I stare up into his beautiful eyes. His eyes dart to the ground as he rubs the back of his neck. "Um, we need to talk" he says uneasily. "No shit" I say and then instantly cover my mouth. Did I really just say that? "Not here though" he says while looking around. "Wait five minutes and then meet me in study room 416." I give him a confused look but nod and turn to go sit on a nearby bench. Did this have to do with his forbidden secrets? Was he in trouble? He must think someone is watching us, so I put on my best poker face and pull out a book to read in the meantime.

When the five minutes are up I stretch and make my way into the library and head to the room. As I approach the room I see Jason staring out the window as he's tapping his pen on the desk. I enter the room and take a seat across from him. I can see the worry in his eyes when he looks at me. "What's wrong?" I ask. "I was afraid this would happen" he says and then pauses before continuing. "After I left your house yesterday, I got a phone call and the voice on the other end told me if I knew what was best, I would leave you alone. They also said that this is warning one of three and I didn't want to find out what would happen when it got to three." My jaw fell open. This is something you hear in a movie, there's no way this is real. "Who was it?" I ask. "Was it Thomas?" I question, instantly becoming furious at the thought of him threatening Jason. "No, Sarah. I don't know who it is. I never do when they call." They? So, it did have to do with Jason's deep dark secrets. "So, what now?" "I told you Sarah. I couldn't deal with thought of someone hurting you because of me. I think the best thing is for us to go our separate ways." I could feel the tears start to swell in my eyes. "I thought you wanted to be with me?" I choke out while holding back the waterfall trying to gush from my eyes. "Come on Sarah. You're making this harder than it already is. You know I want to be with you more than anything, but I would never compromise your safety. Besides, this way you don't have to break Thomas' heart." He says giving me a pitiful half smile. "Since when do you care about how Thomas feels?" I ask. "You're right, I don't, but I know he is good to you, you've told me so yourself. He's not the same jerk he used to be." Now I could see the tears gathering in the corner of Jason's eyes. He tries to grab my hand and I withdraw it back quickly. "Are you sure you aren't just saying this because things happened between you and Stacy and now you don't know how to tell me to back off" I say coldly. "What? No. Why would you think that?" "I saw her wearing your hoodie this morning, and, not to mention how close and giddy she's been acting towards you." "Sarah, no. She got cold on our date last night, so I gave her my hoodie and of course she kept it.

You know how sly girls can be. This morning outside I even told her it was my favorite hoodie and I'd need it back at some point. I don't know why she's acting the way she is. We did have a really nice date, so she probably assumes we are on the tract to dating." "Are you?" I ask, knowing I didn't want to know the answer. "I mean, all things considering, it probably wouldn't be a bad idea. You would be safe and if I could invest myself in a relationship like you have, then it might help me not to lie awake at night driving myself crazy over you." I rise up from my chair, not wanting to hear anymore. My heart ached and my pride was wounded. How do you get broken up with before even dating someone? Jason is probably right, it is for the better. Whatever sketchy trouble he is involved in wasn't worth either one of us risking our life's over. Besides, I can fully devote my feelings into the guy who has been relentlessly dedicated to me and our relationship from the beginning. "Fine." I say and make my way out of the room. I wasn't even in the mood to do homework anymore, so I leave the library and head straight to the gym. I have an hour left until I need to make my way to the field. I decide to pound out some of my frustration on the treadmill to pass some time and help me feel better.

The locker room is loud as it buzzes with excitement while we are getting ready. Music is blaring while most are singing a long while others are listening to Mary in the corner offering her motivational speech, claiming this is going to be *our* season. I forgot how good it feels to have this sense of belonging and meaning. "Alright, alright. Let's settle down" coach Johnson says as he enters the locker room. He starts rattling off the starting lineup and my head whips in his direction when I hear my name called. No way! I made the starting lineup for the first game of the season against a team that they lost to last year, if that isn't a confidence boost, I don't know what is. "Now everyone gather 'round and put your hands in" coach says waiting for everyone to put their hands in before continuing. "Let's go out there and kick some ass, Spartan's on three. One, two, three." The locker room erupts as we throw our hands in the air and then make our way to the field.

Wow. As I look in the stands, I see my grandparents amongst the other fans waving fanatically so I give them a smile and wave. My eyes continue scanning the bleachers and to my hearts content I see Jason clapping to our entrance onto the field. He gives me a smile and I shoot him one back, letting him know I am happy he still came. The mens team is already on the sidelines because they are forced to watch the first half our games to show their support. Not a lot of people come to watch women sports, that's just a saddening fact but I think forcing them to watch if they don't want to, is even more sad. Thomas jogs up to me. "Good luck beautiful even though I know you don't need it." "Thanks and guess what" I say to him. "What?" "I made the starting lineup!" I say excitedly. "Babe that's awesome! I'm so happy for you" he says. "Thank you. I'm gonna go start warming" I say as I jog off to join the rest of the team.

The game was intense, and the opposing team gave us a pretty good run for our money. Right before half time I made the second goal to break our tied score of 1-1. I felt proud going into half time knowing we were winning so far because of the two points I managed to score. By the end of the game, we managed to come out on top and win the game. We finished the game 3-2, thanks to Audry, our striker, getting the winning goal. As we are celebrating our victory, I feel a tap on my shoulder. When I turn around, I see Thomas holding a bouquet of flowers. "These are for you" he says as he hands them to me. "You played amazing" he says. "Thank you" I reply and start to blush as I hear the other girls 'ooh and awe.' "I'm just forewarning you, I didn't buy you any flowers" I say. Thomas laughs, "that's okay I'd take time with you over flowers any time." "You are too sweet sometimes" I say, giving him an exaggerated eye roll. He laughs again, "well now it's my turn to go warm up. I'll see you afterwards right?" "Duh." I say and he gives me a quick kiss on the cheek before trotting onto the field.

I continue my way to the locker room but I am stopped once more. "Hey kiddo, great job out there." "Thanks grandpa. I'm glad you two could make it." "Of course, sweetie!" My grandma says as she gives me a hug. "How about we get a picture?" Grandpa insists while fumbling with the camera. "Would you like me to take a picture for you?" Jason asks as he approaches us. "Jason that would be so kind of you!" Grandma exclaims. After grandma finally approves of the photo Jason takes, she insists that we take a photo together. If it wasn't for our conversation earlier this whole situation wouldn't be so difficult. I can't lie, it felt good being close to him even if this would be for the last time. Jason is almost a foot taller than me so, I always liked the way our heights matched up. Jason puts his arm along my shoulders and I put my arm around his waist, and he pulls me closer, eliminating the awkward gap I tried leaving between us. "Okay, say cheese" grandma says. "Cheese" we sing in unison. "Got it! Oh, Ralph look how adorable it turned out" "Mhm" he says giving it an approving nod as he squints to see. "Well, um, I guess I'll see you at Thomas's later?" "Uh, yeah, I need his address though" Jason says. "I can text it to you." "No. You'll need to send it to Stacy that way it doesn't look like we are trying to meet up." "You've got to be kidding me." I say, but the look on his face tells me it is not a joke. "Alrighty then." I didn't want to argue or get emotional in front of all these people, so I just left it at that. "Okay, thanks" he says. I didn't have anything else to say to him, so I turn to my grandparents and tell them my plans for the night and reassure them that I will be careful. I finally make it to the locker room to shower and change. Once I'm finished I put all my gear in my car and grab some food at the concession stand. I was able to catch the end of the guys game, who were able to pull out a win of 2-1. Looks like it was a good night for both the ladies and the guys team. I make my way to the field to return the congratulations to Thomas. Thomas gives me a bright smile as he sees me approach him. "You played great babe" I say. He moves towards me with his arms outstretched. "Don't you dare" I say sternly while taking a step back. He gives me a mischievous grin as he grabs me into a sweaty hug. "Ugh Thomas, I already showered!" We both start laughing and when our eyes meet he gives me a long kiss before releasing me from his hold. "I'm gonna go shower and get changed but you're welcome to go ahead and head to my place." He says. "Okay, just don't take forever" I tell him. "Oh, does that mean someone is missing me?" "Maybe" I say and give him a kiss before he trots off to the locker room.

As I pull up to Thomas' I see people carrying in kegs and another group unloading speakers. I wonder if his parents actually agreed to this or if they just happen to be out of town. My thought is quickly answered as I see Mr. and Mrs. Carter coming out the front door with suitcases. "Well hello Sarah." Thomas's dad says. "Hi David, hi Teresa." "How'd the games go?" Teresa asks." "We both won" I say proudly. "Alright!" David says as he offers a high five. "Going on a trip?" I ask while nodding towards their luggage. "Unfortunately. We have a meeting in Chicago tomorrow afternoon so duty calls." David states. "So… you are okay with Thomas throwing a party while you're gone?" I ask. They both laugh. "Well you all are adults. All we ask is people respect our property and act responsibly." "We actually prefer to be gone when he throws his parties, so we don't have to listen to all the ruckus" Teresa adds. "Good point" I say as I let out a chuckle. "We better get going though. Have fun and tell our boy we're proud of him." "I sure will" I say as I give each of them a hug goodbye.

Thomas didn't arrive for another 20 minutes later, but that didn't stop the party from starting. By time Thomas made it here, about 40 people already occupied the house and a makeshift DJ had started blasting music. "There's my beautiful girlfriend" Thomas says as he surprises me by hugging me from behind. "About time" I say. He gives me a soft kiss. "I'm starving let's go see what's in the kitchen" he says as he tugs me in the direction of the kitchen. Thomas makes himself a hot dog and offers me a bite first. "Eww no way. Not with mustard on it." I say while shaking my head in disgust. "Ah so you're a ketchup kind of girl." He teases. "Got a problem with that?" I say while crossing my arms. "Hmm, no I think I'll live if I have to give up mustard for you." I let out a giggle at how cute he is being. Thomas grabs himself a beer and starts washing down his hot dog. "So, you're not even going to offer me a drink? How rude." I say teasingly. He raises an eyebrow at me, "I thought you said you couldn't see yourself ever drinking again?" Wow. It's reassuring to know Thomas actually listens to what I tell him. "Beer doesn't affect me as much as liquor does and I don't plan on getting in a car anytime soon." "Well…okay" he says hesitantly as he hands me a beer. "I'm sure we have soda in the fridge that I can grab you instead, if you'd like?" "Babe. It's fine. Trust me, I wouldn't drink if I didn't feel comfortable." "Alright babe," he says while giving me a kiss on the forehead. The beer did help loosen me up because it had been awhile since I had been to such a big party. The amount of people and drunken chaos is bit over-whelming but after my second beer I am starting to feel more at ease. As the night progresses, we found ourselves in the garage playing a game of beer pong.

"I know we're on a roll and all babe, but I need to pee. You can have someone take my spot." I tell Thomas. "Seriously? You're the reason we're winning." "I'll be back" I say. "Do you need me to come with you?" Thomas asks. "No, I think I can handle it" I say giving him a wink. I make my way to the bathroom. I couldn't deny it, I was feeling pretty good with my slight buzz. It's a relief that I'm not wasted right now. I was afraid I had lost my alcohol tolerance since it had been so long since I last drank but so far, so good. I finish my business in the bathroom and attempt to push my way back to the garage. As I'm making my way through the living room I see something that makes me stop dead in my tracks. I feel my heart sink right to the bottom of my stomach right as the sting from the lump in my throat made itself known. Across the way I can see Jason and Stacy making out. It was clear he didn't take long to move on. Screw him, I had Thomas anyway. I'm not sure how long I had been watching them, but when I hear a guy yell 'shots' to the right of me, it snaps me back to reality and suddenly I find myself downing two shots of Tequila back to back. "Shit" I say while shaking my head. I forgot how unpleasant Tequila tasted but at least now my throat burned from the shots and not the lump in my throat.

I continue my journey to the garage, taking another shot that is offered along the way. When I finally make it to Thomas, I could start to feel the heaviness in my head come on. "Heyyy babe" I say. "Hey cutie, what took you so long?" "Oh ya, know" I say before breaking into a giggle fest. "I taked, I mean took. I took some shots." I could feel my words slurring as they came out. "Babe, are you okay?" He asks while coming over to me to steady my balance. "Pfft. I'm great. I mean I would be a lot better if you were kissing me right now" I say. He gives a curious smirk and then kisses me. "Gross. Tequila, really?" "You have no room to talk mustard boy. Besides that's all they had" I reply, which makes him laugh. I'm not sure if the alcohol was getting to me or if it's from being up close to Thomas, but it dawned on me how attracted I am to him. He may not have blue eyes or a heart melting smile, but he is very handsome. I discover the beauty in his light brown eyes as I realize they possess golden specks that entrance me just for a moment, until the weight of the alcohol hits me all at once. "Thomas, the room is spin-

ning" I whisper. "It's okay. I got you babe" he says while picking me up

in one swoop. I loop my arms around his neck and bury my head into his

chest. I could feel him pushing his way through the now very crowded

party and up the stairs. I feel him lay me on his bed, but I cling onto his

shirt, not wanting him to leave. "Don't go," I whisper as I lean up to kiss

him. Thomas kisses me back as he climbs onto the bed and it doesn't

take long before our kisses turn sloppy and our hands start to roam. I

pull my shirt off and then pull off Thomas' shirt. "Damnit" Thomas says

frustratingly as he pulls away from me and starts to put his shirt back on.

I sit up. "What's wrong? Is it me?" I ask, suddenly feeling self-conscious

and trying to use my arms to cover my exposed front half. "Absolutely

not" Thomas says as he kneels down in front of me. "You are so beauti-

ful and you have no idea the things I want to do to you right now, but

you are drunk and it's not right to take advantage of you." I start to cry.

Cue the cry baby drunk Sarah. "Why are you so good to me?" "Because

you deserve all the good things this world has to offer" he tells me. "You

deserve someone better Thomas" I say as the guilt hits me. "Don't you

say that. You are just what I want. Now come on babe lets lay down"
Thomas says. He pulls a shirt from his dresser and helps me put it on before climbing back into bed and snuggling up right next to me. That's
the last thing I remember before I pass out.

Chapter 12

As the sun floods Thomas' room, waking up becomes inevitable.
As I sit up I could feel my head pounding and I let out a groan. Why did
I take those shots last night? I knew I would only regret it when I woke
up with a lovely hangover this morning. Where was Thomas? I get up
and put my clothes back on before I start wandering around what seems
to be a vacant house. I check the clock and I have an hour until my class
starts. Surprisingly I didn't sleep in and miss it. I make my way downstairs and as I look around you wouldn't even think there was a raging
party here last night. The house is spic and span with not a thing out of
place. As I get closer to the kitchen I can smell the sweet aroma of
breakfast and it has my mouth watering.

"Good morning Thomas." "Good morning babe" Thomas says as
he gives me a kiss on the forehead. "You hungry? I thought I'd make us

breakfast before we need to get to school." "I am starving" I reply while rubbing my belly. He laughs "well good. I got some French toast and bacon and the coffee is almost finished brewing." "My, my Thomas. I didn't realize you were quite the food connoisseur." "I've always enjoyed cooking" he says proudly. "In fact, if soccer doesn't work out, I wouldn't mind becoming a chef." "I think I could live with that" I say while pouring myself a decent sized cup of coffee, hoping to relieve some of the throbbing in my head. "There's ibuprofen in the bathroom cabinet, if you need it." It's like he could read my thoughts or something. "Ugh. Thank you. And, um, thank you for last night. I'm sorry if I ruined your party." "Babe, you're fine. Once I knew you were safe and asleep, I locked my door and came back down to put a wrap on the party. It was getting late for a school night anyway." "I just feel bad. I could tell you were having a good time." "I was having a good time, because you were here with me. Besides the only thing you should feel bad for is that, now I'm addicted to waking up next to you and I don't know how I'm gonna cope" he says. I give him a blushing smile. "You are too cute" I say and then head to grab the medicine. Once we finish breakfast,

Thomas offers to drive us to school, but I could imagine my grandparents are worried sick, so I tell him I should probably drive myself, so I can head straight home after class.

Jason isn't in class and it made it hard to focus, but I manage to fumble through and complete one of the projects we are supposed to submit. After class I head to the gym, in hopes of sweating out some of the toxins I polluted my body with last night. As I emerge from the changing room, I spot Jason on the other side lifting weights. I never seen him in a tank top before, and my did it emphasize his broad shoulders and it was driving me crazy wondering what he looked like with it off. The image of him and Stacy making out flashes across my mind and I decide to swallow my pride and go say high.

He sees me approaching in the mirror and turns around and takes out his headphones. "What do you want Sarah?" He says coldly. "Um, wow, okay. Rude, I was just coming to say hi." "Okay. Hi." He says and then turns to continue lifting the weights he had. "Did I do something to upset you?" He pauses mid lift and sets down the weights before turning to me. "Yes, but it doesn't matter because you are no longer my problem." "Woah. Your problem? What is your deal? For someone who was enjoying sucking face with Stacy last night you sure woke up on the wrong side of the bed this morning." He opened his mouth to say something and then stopped. "At least she didn't wake up in my bed this morning." He finally says. "Excuse me?" I say baffled. "When I saw Thomas carrying you up the stairs, I was worried about you, but when I managed to make it up to his room it was evident you were just fine. Word of advice shut the door before you start having sex with somebody." He says before pushing his way past me. "Jason" I shout, but he grabs his bag off the bench and walks straight out of the gym. Why did he have to see that? Nothing even happened, but he wasn't even going to give me the time of the day to explain. Great. I was hurt just seeing him and Stacy making out, I could only imagine how it felt for him to see me eagerly ripping my clothes off for Thomas. There's nothing I could do about it now, so I hop on the treadmill, once again, trying to release my frustrations. After five miles, I am drenched in sweat and decide to call it a wrap. I make my way to the changing room to shower. When I get out of the shower I see a note laying on top of my clothes. I look around and don't see anyone. I didn't even hear anyone come in. I open the note.

I said stay away. Warning #2.

I was officially spooked and it's not like I could tell anyone. I fold the note back up and shove it in my pocket. Whoever it is, did not want me around Jason, but why? Were they okay with him being around Stacy or is she being forbade as well? Not like I could just walk up to her and ask without having to explain myself. Oh well. It was clear Jason didn't want to be around me anyway, so maybe it's best this is how we parted ways, even if it is a misconception. Maybe it will make it easier on his part by thinking I had moved on. I go to my last class of the day and then head home.

"Are you okay?" My grandma asks me frantically. "Yes grandma, I'm sorry I didn't call. I drank a little too much last night and figured it would be best to not drive." "Well, yes that is a smart choice. You could've called Hector to pick you up." "I didn't think about that, plus it was late. Sorry." "As long as you're okay, that's all that matters." I give her a kiss on the cheek. "I need to get ready for work, but I'll see you tonight." "Okay dear." I take a quick shower and leave for work.

When I arrive at work, the manager is already here conducting interviews. Now that school and the soccer season has started, me and Stacy aren't able to work as much as they need us to. Besides, hiring someone else will allow us to have more off days between the each of us. I go about my business and start counting my till and cleaning off the machines. I see my manager and the interviewee stand up and start making their way towards me. "Hi Beth." I say to my manager as she approaches the counter. "Hello Sarah. I'd like to introduce you to Blake. He's our newest member to the team and he's eager to start. I was wondering if you could start training him today?" "Sure, that's not a problem at all" I say to Beth before turning to Blake, "nice to meet you Blake." I say as I offer a handshake. Blake shakes my hand in return, "Pleasure to meet you Sarah" Blake says in a deep country accent. "Let me see if I can go find a shirt in the back for you Blake." Beth says as she disappears to the back. I've never trained anybody before and I'm not a very good teacher so who knows how well this is going to go. I give Blake an awkward smile, not knowing where to even start. He flashes me a pearly white smile and starts looking around the shop. "I'm gonna be honest, I'm fairly new myself and I've never trained someone, so sorry in advance." I tell him. "Ah, it's no biggie. I usually catch on pretty quick anyway." "Here we go!" Beth says excitedly as she remerges from the back. "You said extra large right?" Beth asks Blake. "Sure did. Thanks," he replies as he takes the shirt from her. "Well congratulations and welcome aboard Blake. I've got to get going but I'm leaving you in good hands. Thanks again Sarah!" Beth says as she grabs her papers and heads out the door.

It doesn't take long to show him around and explain the process of what we do. Since the flow is pretty slow and steady I went ahead and let him start ringing people up as I talk him through it. "I think you're doing great" Blake says after about three hours. "Huh?" "You said you never trained anyone, but I think you're doing a great job." "Oh, right. Thanks" I tell him. He leans up against the counter and crosses his arms over his chest. For it being his first day he seems pretty relaxed and at ease with himself. This is when I first take his appearance into account. He is tan and very buff, which is why he needed an extra-large shirt. He has sandy blonde hair that is clean cut with a part down the side that is complimented by his hazel eyes. I'd say he's about 25 or 26 and I couldn't help but get a mysterious vibe from him. "So where are you from? I can't place the accent" I say. "Texas." "Oh cool. How long have you been in California?" I ask. "About a week or so. How about you?" he asks. "Three months give or take." "Ah, looks like I'm not the only one out here for a fresh start" Blake says. "Nope, sorry to burst your bubble" I say jokingly. I didn't want to ask any more details as to why he came here because I didn't want to have to explain myself in return. "Do you plan on enrolling in college?" I ask, changing the subject. "Nah. School's never really been my thing. Besides, I'm an aspiring journalist and I feel like true writers don't need a piece of paper to deem them qualified." It was hard to imagine the big buff guy in front of me who looks like he could be a bodybuilder or security guard was interested in something as soft as writing. "Wow. That's awesome" "Yeah it would be more awesome if I could find a place that would take me on though." "Oh, right. I forget that is a pretty competitive job field." "You can say that again" he says. The rest of the shift we make small talk and when it comes time to close, I show him how everything is supposed to be done and it seems as if he has a pretty good handle on it. It isn't a hard job to learn, but he did catch on pretty quick. I figure after tomorrow he will be good to go on his own. Blake and I exchange numbers and I tell him when to meet me tomorrow, but as I try to part ways Blake insists he walks me to my car because 'a pretty lady shouldn't be walking alone at night'. It's a sweet gesture, but I sure hope this isn't his way of expressing his interest in me. Blake is attractive and all but I just got out of a love triangle, I don't think I could handle another one. Once I get to my car, I decide to text Stacy and give her a heads up that we have a new coworker.

The next day, we just go through the motions doing the same ole same ole, until about five. I'm showing Blake how to refill the machines when the door chime rings. When we turn to greet the customer, I see Stacy and Jason entering the shop. "Hi welcome to Frozen Swirl" Blake says. "Oh, hey Stacy." I say, purposefully ignoring Jason's presence. I could see Jason sizing up Blake and his clenched jaw let me know that he was jealous. "Stacy, this is Blake." I say introducing the two of them.

"Hi Stacy" Blake says in his sweet southern accent. "Well you are not what I pictured when Sarah told me about you" Stacy says as she gives him a wave. Blake looks at me, "wow, I already have a pretty lady telling her friends about me." "Well actually Stacy works here with us." "Ah I see." "Where are my manners?" Stacy interjects, "this is my boyfriend, Jason." Boyfriend, wow that was quick moving. "Nice to meet ya Jason." Blake says giving Jason a nod. Jason nods in return. "I didn't realize you two were dating" I say, not being able to hold it in. "Jason just asked me last night." Stacy says giddily as she loops her arms around Jason's. "Congratulations you two." I say giving them my best smile, but on the inside wanting to break down and cry. "We better get going Stacy. I don't want to get stuck in the rain." "Alright babe. See you guys later." Stacy says giving another wave.

A few minutes after they leave, Blake finally breaks the silence. "So, who broke whose heart?" "Excuse me?" I ask confused. "Did you break Jason's heart, or did he break yours?" "First of all, I have no idea what you're talking about and secondly, that wouldn't be any of your business anyway." Blake just stares at me for a couple seconds. "I forgot to tell you, I specialize in investigative journalism and a big part of it is being able to read people and bring things to light." "So?" I say. "So, I know you're lying. Something happened between the two of you." "Like I said, none of your business." "Okay, whatever you say." Who did this guy think he was? It's only his second day knowing me and he's trying to act like he knows everything about me. Regardless if it's true or not, who says that to a person they just met? I feel my phone buzz and it's a message from Stacy.

You didn't tell me he's a hunk!

It's not right for me to judge, especially since I was leading on two guys up until two days ago, but, she knows Jason is my friend, why would she tell me that. I don't respond and shove my phone back in my pocket. "Is that Jason?" "Dude, really?" "It's just a question." "No, it's not. It's Stacy and she thinks you're a hunk by the way. Happy now?" I say sarcastically. We both stand there looking at each other. "Sorry" he says quietly. "I mean why do you even care?" I ask. "I don't. You two are evidently into each other and I was just wondering why you two weren't together." This guy is a complete stranger and I don't even think

I could fully trust him, but I was in need of a good vent session and he was the only one not involved in the situation, so, I tell him. I don't tell him everything, but I tell him the short and sweet, gist of it all. I didn't mention Jason's suspicious personal life and scary warnings because I didn't know this guy and for all I knew he could be one of the people watching Jason. When I finish explaining my relationship crisis, all Blake had to say is "You have boyfriend?" "Uh, yes…" "Well that's a shame." So, he has been hitting on me. "How so?" I ask. "Because that means I can't ask you on a date." "I don't even know you, what makes you think I'd go on a date with you?" "Isn't the whole point of a date, to get to know a person?" He has a valid point and now I look like an ass. "Touché, but, that doesn't mean we can't get to know each other just as friends." "And how'd that work out for you and Jason?" This guy was relentless, but at least he told it how it is. "Well, I'm trying to change my ways" I scoff. He lets out a light chuckle, "fine, I'll quit pressing the is-sue but just know the minute Thomas slips up, you better believe I'll be there to catch you." I can't believe we just met yesterday, and this guy is already trying to pull moves on me. "I'll keep that in mind" I say. The

rest of the shift goes okay. We make more small talk in between customers and when it comes time to close, Blake insists he do it all so that
he could prove he is ready to be on his own.

When he is finished we lock up and he walks me to my car once
again. Just as we approach my car he grabs my hand but before he can
say anything, I hear a familiar voice shout, "let go of her." My head
snaps quickly in the direction of the voice. "Jason, what are you doing
here?" I ask. "I was coming to talk to you, privately." Jason says as he
looks at Blake. "Well buddy, I don't think you get that pleasure" Blake
responds, "besides, where's your girlfriend?" I could see Jason's hands
clench into a fist. "This doesn't concern you, 'buddy'" Jason says. "I
think it does concern me if you are interfering with my time with Sarah."
"She has a boyfriend" Blake lets out a slight laugh, "yeah I know, and it
isn't you." "Alright can everyone just shut up. This is so awkward that
it's making me cringe just listening to you two. Goodnight Blake. Goodnight Jason" I say and then get into my car. I didn't want to stand here
and listen to two guys fight over me or whatever it is they think they are
doing. Who did they think they are? They think they can just mess with

my mind and my emotions and not take how I feel into consideration. I guess being in a long-term relationship with Jake, I never had the luxury of realizing how frustrating guys can be.

As I drive off, I can see the two of them bickering. I hope that they'll be civil without my presence, but I wasn't going to stand there and hear them hash out their feelings for me and assert their masculinity. Jason made his decision, so why would he bother coming to talk to me. Not too mention, this new guy Blake, how can a guy be so forward in his feelings after two days of knowing someone. Just as I make it home, I receive a text message from an unknown number. *Stay away from Blake.* I try to respond, but the message is blocked from going through. I am pretty sure it was Jason though.

Chapter 13

I spend the next few weeks focusing on school, work, and soccer. I do my best to steer clear of Blake and Jason. It is a weird feeling not sitting next to Jason in class and not talking to him anymore. He was my first friend here and my best friend at that. I wish we could have at least maintained our friendship but we both knew that would only cause more problems. I feel bad, but I even distanced myself from Stacy. She didn't do anything wrong, but being around her and hearing her stories about her and Jason would only make things harder for me. Me and Thomas went on a couple dates here and there, but with soccer and other responsibilities in the way we haven't ben able to hang out as much as we want to. I could feel myself becoming a hermit again and it didn't help the anniversary of Jake's death was approaching. As I sat in my room twirling the ring my, would have been fiancé gave me that awful night, all I want to do is cry and fade away into the darkness of the night. I haven't felt this angry or emotional since the first two months following the accident. I can't tell if it is from the realization that it has been almost a whole year without Jake or the fact that I screwed things up with the one person that I managed to fall in love with. This is the first time I have allowed myself to entertain the thought that I love Jason, but it makes since. I am miserable without him in my life, no matter how sweet or loving Thomas is, my mind and heart can't help but long for Jason. I told myself after Jake died, I would never love again, I didn't deserve to. Besides, I never thought I would be capable of loving again. There was nothing I could do about losing Jake, but there is something I can do about losing Jason. I need to tell him how I feel, I just don't know how without drawing attention to the people that are watching Jason.

I have an idea and although it might make me one of the worst people in the world, I'm going to allow myself to be cheated from happiness once again. I text Stacy to use her as the middle-man.

Hey Stacy, is Jason okay? I haven't been able to get ahold of him and we were supposed to meet at the pier to go over a project.

I was hoping she would relay the message to him and he would get the hint. My phone buzzes.

Hmm, that's unlike him. I'll ask and tell him to text you.

I was now pacing my room. I know he wouldn't actually text me, but if he got the hint he would know to meet at our special spot under the pier. Only question is how long do I wait before I head there? I want him to get there first so I can see if anybody is watching him.

I wait an hour before I leave for the pier and by time I pull up its midnight and there aren't many people here. Which means it'll be easy to spot any sketchy looking people lingering around. I can feel my heart start to beat faster with each step. It has been about three weeks since I last spoke to Jason and it makes me feel excited and nervous all at the same time to see him and talk to him again. What if he doesn't feel that same way about me anymore? I don't know how close him and Stacy have gotten over these past few weeks. When I make it to the pier, I can see Jason down below, staring out into ocean. I could feel my heart start to flutter as I stood there watching him. I quickly start scoping out the perimeter around the pier. I don't see anyone, so I throw away the rest of my pretzel and make my way back down the pier. I knew he would get the hint.

When I make it down below, he is still staring out into the abyss and I stop a few feet away. He hasn't noticed me yet and I don't know how to approach him. Do I just tap him on the shoulder? Should I call out his name? I take too long to decide because Jason turns around and sees me. "Sarah" is all he says. I lose it and I run to him and jump into his arms, burying my face into his neck as I start to cry. I wrap my legs around his waist as he carries me under pier, shielding us from possible onlookers. "What's wrong? Are you okay?" He asks me frantically as he sets me down looking for signs of injury. Little did he know, it was my heart that was hurt. "No" I manage to choke out behind the tears. "Who hurt you?" He says angrily. "You did." He gives me a puzzled expression. "Me?" He questions. "I love you and you just turned me away like you didn't even care anymore. The last few weeks have been terrible without you and it's made me realize I don't want to spend another day not having you in my life." Probably not the most romantic way to tell someone you love them, but my rambling is put to a stop as Jason presses his lips to mine, reassuring me that he still feels the same way. Jason pulls away. "I love you too Sarah. I've been miserable without you." I embrace him and look up into his blue eyes and right then and there I know I want to give him my whole heart. There is something about loving him that felt familiar, it felt right. I pull Jason into another kiss and it makes me feel more alive. I can smell his cologne as it lingers in the air between us and with each inhale it only made me want more. Our kisses become more passionate and it sends a tingly sensation throughout my entire body. It was evident my heart wasn't the only thing that missed

Jason. My body had been craving his touch and from the goosebumps on Jason's arms, I would say the feeling was mutual. He pulls away and looks me in the eyes. "Run away with me" he says. "What?" I ask, confused. "We can't be together here. If we leave then we won't have to worry about staying away from one another. I know it's a lot to ask and that it's a huge risk, but I promise I will take care of you." I stare into his mesmerizing blue eyes as I listen to him talk and I determine there's no way I could lose true love a second time. "Lets go!" I blurt out, cutting him off. He gives me a shocked expression as if he wasn't expecting me to agree. "Really?" Jason asks. I nod my head excessively as I wipe away my happy tears. "Give me your phone" he demands. I hand it to him and watch him as he starts typing. He hands it back to me, "this is my address. Pick me up at seven in the morning. This way we can both pack our things and you can let your grandparents know." "Okay" I say excitedly. "Now go. I will head up the other way" he tells me. I nod and he gives me another kiss before we part ways.

As I make my way back to my car, I can feel my heart fluttering. The thrill of running away with the guy I love has me excited and anxious all at the same time. What if the people come looking for us, or even worse tries to hurt or kill us? How are my grandparents going to take it? I would have to tell my parents and Haley. I would be dropping out of school once again and they will be so disappointed. Poor Thomas. Would I tell him anything or just leave without a trace? I make my way home and when I arrive, I head straight to my room to pack. Fortunately, I didn't bring much with me when I moved from Kentucky, so I am able to consolidate all my belongings into two suitcases. It's too late to talk to my grandparents so I will have to wait till the morning to do so. I lay down to get some sleep, but my adrenaline rush makes it difficult to do so. Where were we going to go? Did this mean I would be considered a criminal now? One thing is for sure, Jason will have to tell me his big secret.

Chapter 14

I'm not sure what time I fell asleep but when my alarm clock rings, I jolt out of bed. I quickly get dressed and carry my suitcases downstairs. I set them in the entryway and make my way into the kitchen to face my grandparents. "Hi grandpa" I say. He puts down his newspaper and looks at this watch. "My Sarah, you are up early." I let out a nervous laugh as I start to fiddle with my hands. He cocks his head at me and motions at the chair across from him. "Why don't you sit and tell me what's on your mind sweet pea." I sit down. "Where's grandma? She should be here too." "She left last night for a project" my grandpa replies. "Oh, right." He grabs my hand and looks me in the eyes, "is everything okay darlin?" I couldn't waste too much time or I will be late. "Grandpa, I need to tell you something and I hope that you will support me and not try to talk me out of this." "Go on" he says. "Me and Jason want to run-away together. I know it sounds crazy, but there's certain reasons why we can't be together if we stay here." He remains silent as he rubs his chin. "I love him Grandpa and I didn't expect any of this, but it just hap-pened, and I don't want to live without him." "Is Thomas threatening you or him?" Grandpa asks. "No! Thomas would never. To be honest I can't tell you as to why, just that Jason's past keeps him from being free." "I see" grandpa says. There's not much else for me to say so we sit in silence. "Will you be in danger?" Grandpa finally asks. Even I didn't know the answer but I need my grandpa's support on this. "Not if we leave" I tell him. "Very well. You are old enough to make your own decisions and it would be wrong of me to stand in the way of your happiness. However, you will need to tell your parents, it is not my place to tell them such things." I jump up from my chair and give him a hug and a kiss on the cheek. "Thank you for understanding grandpa." "Where will you two go? Do you need money?" "I'm not sure where we are going yet, we just decided last night and no I can't take anymore of your money grandpa." "Follow me" he motions. He leads me to their room and into his closet. "You will need more money than you think and if people are watching you, then you will need to pay with cash until you two can get new cards." Grandpa then opens a safe and pulls out five stacks of bills. "This is five thousand dollars, spend it wisely" he says. My mouth drops open as I try to hand back the money. "Grandpa I can't take this." "You can, and you will." I give him another hug, "thank you grandpa. I will never be able to repay you." I look at the clock on his wall. "Go" he says, "and be safe, I love you sweet pea." "I love you too" I say before turning and rushing back downstairs.

I pull up to the apartment complex fifteen minutes till seven and park my car. I can feel my excitement raging. As seven approaches there is no sign of Jason. Maybe he is still getting his stuff ready. I refrain from texting him because I don't want to give away our plan. When it turns 7:30 and there is still no sign of Jason, I can't sit still any longer. I get out of the car and make my way to his apartment. When I approach his door, I knock, but there is no answer. I try turning the knob and the door opens so I let myself in. The place is bare and simple, no decorations and just the essentials. I venture further into the apartment and I can't help but let out a gasp as I enter the bedroom. There's blood on the comforter of the neatly made bed with a note laying on top. I slowly make my way to the side of the bed and pick up the piece of paper. *I warned you. Now you'll never see him again.* I let the note fall from my hand as I start to tremble. Did they kill Jason? Should I call the cops? I begin to cry. What am I supposed to do now? I can't call the cops, what would I say? I would have to explain everything to them and that would mean exposing Jason. I pull out my phone and try to text Jason but receive an error message in return. I don't know what to do, so I call the only person that I know that might be capable of helping me.

"Hello." "Oh Blake, I'm so glad you answered. I need your help" I say. "What's up buttercup?" "If I text you an address can you meet me here?" "Ooh I like the way this sounds." "Blake, this is serious. Please." "Okay, okay, sorry. Send me the address and I'll be there." I hang up and text him the address. I spend the next hour waiting for Blake to arrive by snooping around the apartment trying to find some sort of clue as to who could be behind this and why they are so desperate to keep me and Jason apart. I discover a journal behind Jason's nightstand. The first entry is dated ten months ago and reads,

Like most nights, I can't sleep. I guess I can't complain, I would rather lay awake than see the nightmares. I read online that writing your thoughts down can help a person overcome their fears and help reveal your inner conscious, so here I am. I am desperate to make the thoughts stop, they are driving me insane. I see her face every time I close my eyes and even in my dreams. A part of me feels love for this mystery woman and that's probably why it hurts me to see her die each night in my dreams. Ever since my accident, I can't remember anything from be-

fore. Did I kill this beautiful woman that causes me to lay awake each night?

The next entry is dated on my second day here in Los Angeles,

I can't believe it! I met the girl from my dreams today. She is even more beautiful in person. Her name is Sarah. Is this fate or are my nightmares a prophecy, warning me to stay away? I can't help but want to get to know her. I told mom about her and she was not happy, she told me to stay away. I don't get why she has to be so over protective all the time. I didn't ask for any of this, I'll never understand why she had to ...

A sharp knock on the front door startles me, bringing me back to reality. I check the peep hole first and see Blake. I let him in. "Hey, thanks for coming." "No problem. Uh what are you doing here?" He asks. "What do you mean?" "Uh, nothing. I just meant, I thought you lived with your grandparents?" "I do. This is Jason's apartment." "Ah. He says as his eyes start to dart around the apartment." "Jason is missing, and I think some bad people either hurt him or plan on killing him. I need your help finding him." Blake's eyes gaze to the journal in my hand. "What is that?" He asks. "It's Jason's journal, I found it just before

you got here." He snatches it from me. "Hey give that back!" I yell.
"You shouldn't be here" he hisses. "What are you talking about?" "You
need to leave" Blake says. "You know something, don't you?" I ask in-
quisitively. "I don't know what you're talking about" he says as he turns
to leave. I grab his arm, "please Blake." I start to cry. "I've already lost
one person I love. I don't know if I'd be able to handle losing another." I
drop to the floor and begin to sob. Blake kneels down next to me, "why
didn't you listen to the warnings?" "You know about the warnings?" I
ask surprised. I don't remember telling him about the threats. "I know
about a lot of things" he says. "How?" I reply. "I need you to tell me
something" Blake says ignoring my question. "What?" I ask. "How did
Jake die?" The question throws me off and I give him a confused look.
"What does Jake have to do with this?" "Please, Sarah. I need to know
I'm doing the right thing."

"Well, that night I was at a party. I shouldn't have been at that stupid party." I say angrily as I shake my head. "Jake was supposed to pick
me up from my parent's house, he had a surprise for us planned that
night, but I had too much to drink at the party. Jake had to come pick me

up since I was careless and became too drunk to drive. By time Jake showed up we were running late for the reservations he made. He told me we had a bit of a drive so I should take a nap so I could be refreshed for when we got there. When I woke up, we had been in an accident. At that point we were both alive and were able to call for help. While we were waiting, I lashed out at Jake for taking us out, when really, it was my fault for drinking and not making our plans the priority. That's when he revealed his plans of proposing to me that night." I say as I retrieve the necklace from my pocket. "The first car that rear-ended us pushed us into the intersection which allowed the second car to t-bone us on Jake's side. By time we got to the hospital, Jake was in critical condition, fighting for his life. They were trying to suction all the blood out of his mouth when he coded. There were so many people surrounding him, shouting, check for a pulse, resume compressions, push the epi. I remember hearing the horrible flat line tone just before they rushed him off. I would've given anything to trade places with him. He didn't deserve to die." "I am so sorry" Blake says as he tries to grab my hand, but I instantly pull away. "Are you happy now?" I say wiping away the tears running down my face. "Now tell me about Jason" I demand. Blakes lowers his tone to a whisper, "Jason, isn't who you think he is." "What do you mean?" I ask. "All this is going to sound crazy, but you have to trust me" he says waiting for my nod of approval before continuing. "Jason is Jake." "That's not possible" I yell, angry that Blake would play with my mind and emotions like this. "Let me finish. Jake did not die that night. They were able to bring him back. Ms. Henson paid the doctor to give false information in front of you, so you would think he had died. Then she had him transferred to a hospital out here. I guess she has some friends in the witness protection program who helped her provide a fake death certificate and a new identity for him in case you got suspicious." My head starts to spin and I feel like I could throw up. There is no way this could be true. Besides, what are the odds that we would find each other after thinking each other had died. "Then why doesn't he remember me?" I ask snarkily. "He hit his head pretty hard from what I was told and has been suffering some long term amnesia. That's why Ms. Henson was so quick to move him away, so he wouldn't be able to see familiar things and people that could possibly recall back his memory. That hasn't stopped him from remembering you though, as I'm sure you read in the journal." I sit there, astonished. Would Ms. Henson really go to such lengths to keep us apart?

I remember Ms. Henson coming to the foot of my bed, seeming concerned about my condition for just a moment before the doctor approaches her, giving me a sideways glance, "I'm really sorry" is all he says before Ms. Henson breaks into a sob. "No!" I remember screaming as I lurch forward bursting into tears myself. "Leave it to you to ruin his life once again. Now you'll never see him again." Ms. Henson says before walking off. Leaving me alone, hurt and heart broken.

The longer I pondered over it, the more it started to make sense. She was quick to file a restraining order, as if I would ever want to be near her without Jake around. She held the funeral in secret so that way I would not be able to attend and she never released and obituary. When Jake's father died, he did leave behind a significant amount of money, which would make the funding of all this possible. I have blamed myself everyday for his death. I went through months of crippling depression, countless prescriptions, and many therapist sessions. My blood started to boil as I began to feel nothing but hate for this woman. I want to go right up to her and slap her, confront her, something, anything to release my anger. But wait, this means that she is the one behind keeping us apart, therefore her threats were harmless. She would never actually do anything to her son.

"Where is he?" I ask Blake. I could see the reluctance in his face. "Blake you already screwed up by telling me the truth. Please, I can't lose him again." "It's not that simple. The other guys that watch over him are cold and ruthless and abide by Ms. Henson's rules." "Once I expose the truth…" "No, Sarah, you can't do that. Ms. Henson will never have them harm her son, but that doesn't mean she won't have them do something to you. They can easily kill you and make it look like an accident." "Then I'll go to her and have her confess to me." "Are you crazy?" Blake asks me. "You didn't know?" I say giving him a smirk and snatch the journal back from him before standing up. "I'll be needing this, I say." "She'll just deny it and besides she has a restraining order on you. She'll have the cops called before you can even ring the doorbell." "That's fine, then she can explain herself to the police." "If she doesn't buy herself out of trouble and have them chalk you up as a psychotic ex-girlfriend of her deceased son." He is right. She has probably had this planned out since the beginning. I was getting frustrated. "Well I don't have many options here Blake!" He gives me a look of defeat, "she's sending him to Arizona. He's at the airport now, his flight leaves at 3:45." I look at my phone, it's 8:57. "We need to go!" I say pulling him up, "we can make it if we hurry."

Chapter 15

By time we make it to the airport, it is 2:59. During the ride, I paid Blake to buy two tickets to Kentucky under his name, for me and Jason. We discuss our plan one last time before I make my way to the terminal. Blake will go to the Arizona terminal and somehow tell Jake to meet me at the Kentucky terminal. Blake will then distract the other guys by telling them how I found Jake's journal and was reading it when he confronted me at the apartment. I am praying that he will be able to distract them long enough for us to board the plane. The plane to Kentucky leaves at 4:05 and I am hoping this time lapse doesn't give them enough time to figure out where he might go.

At 3:55 there's still no sign of Jake. I knew it would be a gamble on whether Blake would betray me or not. As the line to board the plane gets shorter, I have no choice but to get in line. "Sarah!" I turn around and see Jason jogging up to me. "You made it" I say. I hand him his ticket to be scanned as we wait to board the plane. It's not until we are on the runway that my nerves finally disappear. I can't believe this plan actually worked.

Jake grabs ahold of my hand and gives it a squeeze. I give him a soft smile. "We have a lot to discuss" I tell him. This isn't going to be easy convincing someone that they aren't who they think they are. It feels bizarre enough believing it myself. "Your name isn't Jason" I say. Jake lets out a chuckle and feels my forehead, "are you feeling okay?" "Look, um, Jason, everything I am about to tell you is going to sound outrageous, but I think once you hear this, things will start to make sense." "Okay..." he says suspiciously. "You are Jake. My Jake, the one I thought I lost. Your mom arranged for you to be sent away after the accident. Which explains why you would see me in your dreams, I wasn't a mystery like you wrote in your journal. You saw me in your dreams because I was a part of your repressed subconscious." I pause letting him register what I have just told him. "Sarah, you realize how crazy that sounds, right?" "Just think about it. Why else would your mom not want us to be together? Your moms name is Mary Henson, right?" His eyes narrow, "yes, how did you know that?" "Because I am telling the truth. Your actual name is Jake Henson and you are from Kentucky. We started dating the summer before sophomore year." I pull out my phone out and show him old pictures of us together before the accident. "See, that's us together!" I push back his shaggy blond hair which reveals a scar on his forehead from where it had hit the steering wheel. How did something as simple as a new hair color and style keep me from recognizing him? I have to admit, it was clever of Ms. Henson, she had really thought it all through. "You proposed to me that night," I say pulling the necklace from my pocket once more and dangling it in between us. "After the accident your mom had you transferred to California and created a new identity for you to live by." Jake leans back into his seat and I can see the confusion and skepticism roaming across his face. "I know this is a lot to take in" I say softly. "It just doesn't make sense." He says frustratingly, "why would she do all this to keep us apart?" "I don't know why she would go to such extremes, but she never liked us together. She would always say I wasn't good enough for you" I reply. "My mom told me that before my accident a girl tricked me into falling in love with her so I would do all her dirty work. She was a drug addict and would have me deliver drugs for her and the night of my accident was a delivery gone wrong because the people she was involved with, thought I stole from them. That's why she faked my accident as a death and told me she was going to place me under protection so no one would be able to hurt me again." My mouth falls open as he tells me this . "She is so full of shit" I say angrily. Of course, she would make me out to seem like some horrible person in order to convince him he was danger and listen to her. "I believe you" he says as he gives my hand another squeeze and offers me his contagious smile. I smile back at him. "So what do we do now?" I ask curiously. Jake takes the ring from my hand, "Well for starters, how about we pick up where we left off?" He says cocking an eyebrow at me as he slides the ring on to my finger. I give him a tearful smile and nod yes. "What are the odds?" I ask him. Jake gives me a passionate kiss and then whispers to me, "love finds a way."

www.ingramcontent.com/pod-product-compliance
Lightning Source LLC
Chambersburg PA
CBHW020909180626
46816CB00007BA/2316